S0-AVT-863

MAX BAER & THE STAR OF DAVID

Also by Jay Neugeboren

MAX BAER & THE STAR OF DAVID

JAY NEUGEBOREN

[M]

Mandel Vilar Press

Copyright © 2016 by Jay Neugeboren

All rights reserved. No portion of this book may be reproduced in any form or by any means, including electronic storage and retrieval systems, except by explicit prior written permission of the publisher. Brief passages may be excerpted for review and critical purposes.

This is a work of fiction. Names, characters, places, and incidents are either the product of the author's imagination or are used fictitiously. Any resemblance to actual persons, living or dead, is entirely coincidental.

This book is typeset in Monotype Sabon. The paper used in this book meets the minimum requirements of ANSI/NISO Z39.48-1992 (R1997). ∞

Designed by Barbara Werden

Portions of this book in somewhat different form have appeared in *Commonweal*, *Jewish Fiction*, and *Blunderbuss*.

Publisher's Cataloging-in-Publication Data

Neugeboren, Jay.
    Max Baer & the star of David / Jay Neugeboren.

        pages ; cm

    Issued also as an ebook.
    ISBN: 978-1-942134-17-6

    1. Baer, Max, 1909–1959—Fiction. 2. Jewish boxers—United States—Fiction. 3. African Americans—Relations with Jews—Fiction. 4. Paramours—Fiction. 5. Incest—Fiction. 6. Biographical fiction. I. Title. II. Title: Max Baer and the star of David

PS3564.E844 M39 2016
813/.54

Printed in the United States of America

16 17 18 19 20 21 22 23 24 / 9 8 7 6 5 4 3 2 1

Mandel Vilar Press
19 Oxford Court, Simsbury, Connecticut 06070
www.americasforconservation.org | www.mvpress.org

for Jerry and Lenore

Contents

Foreword

When, on November 21, 1959, in Garden Grove, California, Max Baer, a former heavyweight champion of the world, died at the age of fifty, my father, Horace Littlejohn, was at his side. Thirty-six years later, on June 11, 1995, in Canastota, New York, when Max Baer was posthumously inducted into the International Boxing Hall of Fame, I was there, standing beside Max Baer's eldest son, my half-brother, Max Baer Jr. By this time, Max Baer Jr., who had no knowledge that I was his blood relation, had become an actor best known for his role as Jed Clamplett's nephew, Jethro Bodine, in the television show *The Beverly Hillbillies* (in which show the ill-fated Sharon Tate, murdered along with four others by followers of Charles Manson, played an employee of Beverly Caterers), and a man as celebrated by the public as his father had been.

I was born on May 30, 1938, a half year after Max Baer Jr. came into this world, and I grew up with him during the years my father was Max Baer's "Man Friday," and my mother, Joleen Littlejohn, was Max Baer's housekeeper and tutor to his children. My parents were people of color, my father's skin a rusty brown-black with tones of violet lending it a slightly luminescent caste, and my mother's coloring, which I had the good fortune to inherit, a rich shade of mocha-brown that, in summer, took on a pale gossamer-thin veil of crimson. Known to one and all as my father Horace's wife, my mother was, in actuality, my father's sister, and it was not until the day I came of age, on May 30, 1956, that she informed me this was so, and that it was Max Baer, and not Horace Littlejohn, who was my biological father. She also, on that day, swore me to secrecy concerning this matter. "Incest," she declared, and with her endearingly mordant wit, "was but an infrequent and rarely talked-about pastime in our family."

She hoped I would understand that although Max Baer acknowledged privately that he had fathered me—thus his liberality in allowing me to be playmate to his children, and his generosity in providing for me an education equal to theirs—it was Horace Littlejohn who was more truly my father, since it was he who, with her, raised me and was instrumental in the cultivation of those skills and values that have enabled me to live a life of not inconsiderable achievement.

Educated at the University of California at Berkeley, the University of Chicago Graduate School, Union Theological Seminary, and Christ College, Oxford, I hold two doctorates (one in classics, and one in medieval European history), along with a master's degree in divinity. I am fluent in Greek, Latin, and Hebrew, and have become a biblical scholar of some note, with two slender, well-received books, and a fair number of published essays, the majority of which concern The Song of Solomon (more accurately, The Song of Songs, Which is Solomon's, although Solomon had no hand in writing it). I have also written extensively on two related texts, Ecclesiastes and The Book of Job, which texts, like The Song of Solomon, remain at odds in theme, content, and philosophy with all other canonical texts, and whose inclusion in the Hebrew and Christian Holy Bibles remains an anomaly that has provided me, as it has other scholars and theologians, with many happy hours of inquiry and speculation.

Despite the rabbinical attempt to transform it into an allegory of God's love for Israel, and Christianity's attempt to transform it into an allegory of Christ's love for the church, The Song of Solomon is, has been, and will ever be a poem in praise of the natural world (God's name, in fact, does not appear in the text), and of physical love between a young man and young woman. That I was, early on, enormously taken with it was doubtless influenced by my mother's extreme devotion to it—to its reveling in the sensual joys of young love—along with the presence, during my childhood and coming-of-age, of Max Baer, who was second to no man or woman I have ever known in his capacity to delight in corporeal pleasures.

As will be seen from the manuscript to which this note is prefatory, I inherited from my father, along with an openness to sybaritic indulgences (my parents, if less visibly or flamboyantly, also sought out and knew, as the document here attached reveals, a considerable range of worldly pleasures), a style of expression some might regard as mannered, but a style—more exactly, a sensibility—that prepared me well for studies in classical rhetoric, and for being able to set down from time to time, with, I trust, a clarity and vividness comparable to his, experiences and thoughts I have deemed worthy of preservation.

In his lifetime, Max Baer was renowned for possessing the most powerful right hand in the boxing world. He was also considered something of a clown, this reputation enhanced by his career in films and in vaudeville (where he performed comical routines with the ex-boxer, "Slapsie Maxie" Rosenbloom). It would be more accurate, however, to see him not as a comic figure but as a man of biblical stature, a claim I do not make lightly. Like King David, Max Baer was a great warrior who represented and advanced the cause of the People of Israel at a time when they were subject to oppression, humiliation, and the threat of annihilation. Like King David, Max Baer was a great admirer and lover of women, and like King David and other biblical figures, beginning with the first patriarch, Abraham, he often loved several women concurrently, his wife included, while fathering children by his wife and others. More: like King David, who declared that his love for King Saul's son, Jonathan, was "wonderful, passing the love of women," Max Baer, too, gloried in his love for another man even while news of that love had the power to bring him low. And like King David, who made a covenant with Jonathan that was to prevail through all generations so that death would never divide them, and who honored this covenant by adopting Jonathan's son Mephibosheth as his own following upon Jonathan's death in battle, Max Baer, in effect, adopted his lover's son, although he did so without formalizing the relationship, or revealing that the son was his own. Like King David, too, Max Baer was responsible, by the exercise of his God-given power, for the deaths of innocent men.

It is now seven years since I passed the proverbial three score and ten, and I have recently received from my physician the unwelcome news that I will not in all probability live to pass three score and ten by a sum of eight. I have therefore completed the preparation of the accompanying text, "The Max Baer I Knew," dictated to my mother by my father before his passing on September 22, 1999, when, his eyesight failing, he could no longer see well enough to set down the story himself, and given to me by my mother before her passing seven months later, on April 17, 1999.

Quotations at the beginnings of chapters, from the King James version of The Song of Solomon, are of my choosing, as are the chapter titles. I have edited the text for minor matters of spelling, punctuation, and consistency, but have changed nothing substantive. I commend it to readers with the words of a common Latin valediction often attributed to Ovid: *finis coronat opus*, which I translate freely as: May a grand work crown a good life!

Here, then, my father's story, in his own words.

HORACE LITTLEJOHN JR.
Sacramento, California
30 May 2015

MAX
BAER &
THE STAR OF
DAVID

1

Star of David

I am come into my garden, my sister, my spouse: I have gathered my myrrh with my spice; I have eaten my honeycomb with my honey; I have drunk my wine with my milk; eat, O friends; drink, yea, drink abundantly, O beloved. (5:1)

I was with Max Baer when he fought and defeated Frankie Campbell and delivered blows that, according to the physician's postmortem, set loose Frankie Campbell's brain from its skull and was the cause of Frankie Campbell's death. I was with him when he fought and defeated Ernie Schaaf in a bout that left Schaaf unconscious; I was with him when he received the news that Schaaf had died during a bout with Primo Carnera; and I was with him when sportswriters, the famed Jimmy Cannon and Grantland Rice among them, reported what many of us, including Max, believed to be true: that Schaaf's death was due to damage previously inflicted by Max. These incidents, which earned Max the reputation of "killer," affected him profoundly—broke his heart, in truth—for there never was, in my experience, a kinder, more gentle man, or one who, when not grieving for men he had hurt (myself included), gloried in life as fully and with as much exuberant love as did Max Baer.

I was with Max when he made the decision, before his bout against Hitler's boxer, Max Schmeling, whom he crushed utterly, to adorn his boxing trunks with the Star of David, an emblem he would wear proudly for the remainder of his boxing career, and I was with him when he defeated the Argentinian behemoth, Primo Carnera, for the heavyweight championship of the world. I was with him, too, when, one day short of a year later, he lost this title to James J. Braddock.

I was with him when he married Dorothy Dunbar (a socialite and actress famous at the time for her role as Jane in an early Tarzan film), and I was with him through their numerous and highly publicized separations and reunions. I attended to him faithfully during his liaisons with some of our loveliest ladies of the silver screen—Greta Garbo, Mae West, and Jean Harlow among them—which liaisons supplied regular copy for the gossip columnists. I was at his side when he married Mary Ellen Sullivan, and with Mary Ellen and Max when each of their children—Max Baer Jr., James Manny, and Maudie Marian—was born—and I was, of course, with my sister Joleen when she gave birth to Max Baer's son, Horace Littlejohn Jr., who, given that I was known to all as Joleen's husband, was assumed to be my son.

On the night we first met Max Baer, as on previous occasions when we were together in public places, Joleen and I employed the fiction that we were husband and wife. We persisted in the deception in this instance so that we might gain employment with Max, and—a prospect dimly sensed, if at all, on that evening—come to live a life marked by privileges known to few whose origins were similar to ours. For while Max Baer's life was the object of much public scrutiny, our domestic life—Joleen's, Horace Jr.'s, and mine—was informed by a dearly cherished sense of privacy, albeit this privacy derived initially from a lamentable but necessary secrecy that, if betrayed, would have cast deadly shadows not only upon our lives, but upon Max Baer's life as well. That we were people of color in the employ of white folks played no small part in our ability to remain private—to not be seen by others—a situation well known to people of color who served white people during that era.

Although Joleen's exceptional beauty and fierce intellect made many men, Max Baer's friends among them, pay her admiring and sometimes lewd attentions (as they did, though with less frequency, to me), in his service we were, for the most part, no more noticeable to others than the brooms, dustmops, laundry baskets, and serving dishes we utilized, a fact Joleen would comment on occasionally, noting, for example, that when, after a bath or shower—or between rounds of a boxing match—I served as Max Baer's towel holder, I was not so different, even to Max himself, from the towel holders secured to bathroom walls except that, she said, I was considerably more mobile. For as kind and generous as Max could be, he was not without a self-absorbed vanity that frequently blinded him not merely to the ways others perceived him, but to the very fact that others existed.

I will speak now of how I met Max Baer on the evening that forever changed my life and that of my sister.

The year was 1929, the day and month, Thursday, October 17, a week before the stock market crash on what would become known as "Black Thursday," and the day upon which Joleen and I celebrated her twenty-first birthday.

Joleen had, the previous spring, received a certificate of graduation from California State Normal College in Alameda, and was working in San Francisco for a wealthy Japanese family as a domestic while she prepared for licensing examinations that would enable her to become a full-time teacher in the public schools of San Francisco. She and I shared a small apartment not far from the Presidio, in a section of the city called Polish Town that, despite its name, was home mostly to recent Russian immigrants, a fair number of them Jewish. I worked as a day laborer, standing in line each morning with others, mostly Asian, though some were of Irish, Spanish, or Negro extraction, in the Mission Bay section of the city, at the corner of Third and Sixteenth Streets, waiting there to be picked up for a day on the docks where I would sort, cut, gut, clean, and box fish. In the evenings, though irregularly, I attended classes at a local public high school in order that I might secure a high school diploma. On days when there was no work, and on evenings when I had no classes, I trained at a local boxing gymnasium, honing skills that had, earlier in life, when Joleen and I lived in Kinnard, Texas, with our parents and siblings (two sisters, three brothers), earned me several amateur titles and, by wagers Joleen placed discreetly on my bouts, enough money to allow us, when Joleen turned seventeen and I was but a month shy of fifteen, to leave home and make our way to California so that, far from our family, who we truly were to each other might not be discovered, for if it had, we would have lost what was most dear to us in the world while bringing down shame, humiliation, and disgrace upon our selves and upon those who loved us and whom we loved.

Throughout the years of my adolescence, notwithstanding the fear and anxiety our intimacy engendered, I was able to benefit from Joleen's knowledge of and sensitivity to language, and from her exquisite skill at being able to transmit this knowledge, though

I was initially resistant to book learning. Like my brothers, of whom I was the youngest, I saw book learning as an essentially female endeavor. In addition, I could not see how, given that I was a man of color, gaining an education, or even a college diploma, would serve as a viable means of making my way in the world. The sure way to do that, I believed, lay in my physical prowess—my strong back, my keen reflexes, my lightness of foot, and, above all, the wicked quickness and strength of my hands, the fingers of which were unnaturally long and which, after my arrival in San Francisco, had earned me the sobriquet "Long-fingered Littlejohn."

This was, in fact, the way Max Baer first addressed me while Joleen and I were eating our dinner on the evening of October 17, 1929.

We had chosen Perfidie, a restaurant on Russian Hill renowned for its elegant French fare and for the fact that its owners, who claimed descent from Russian nobility, spoke to one another and the staff solely in French. Perfidie was also one of the few fine restaurants that did not turn away individuals of color. Although we were, perforce, obliged generally to be frugal, we also, as on this evening, would occasionally pander to our desires out of all proportion to our means and to our station. Joleen, in a silver-gray, full-length, strapless evening dress, her long, black hair held in place by a forest-green silk scarf, was aglow with pleasure, as well as from the effects of champagne, a full bottle of which we had nearly finished before our entrées arrived. I wore white linen slacks and—Joleen's gift to me for my nineteenth birthday—a matching long-sleeved white linen shirt with barrel cuffs. Although the restaurant prided itself on the legend that Perfidie was a place where, as in Paris, married individuals could have romantic dinners with companions to whom they were not married, and do so without creating unwelcome gossip or scandal, my own sense was that Joleen and I were perhaps the only couple there that evening whose intimate life had anything in common with the restaurant's name or legend.

"You're 'Long-fingered Littlejohn,' ain't you?" Max Baer said when he came to our table.

"I am," I said. "And who might you be?"

Max turned a chair around and, straddling it, rested his large forearms upon the chair's back.

"I'm Max Baer," he said, "and I'm a fighter too, hey—won all five of my professional fights so far, four by knockout. I heard about you at Silvio's, where I work out, and I'm in the market for a sparring partner with quick hands."

"While it's true that I have at times trained at Silvio's," I said, "I have recently made a decision not to enter the ring, either as an amateur or professional, for the foreseeable future."

"Whoa Nelly," Max said. "You got some fancy gift of gab for a nigger. You didn't pick up lingo like that in any ring I been in, I can tell you that much. But hey—I can pay you good. I got money rolling in these days, with more coming."

"The allure of monetary gain will not affect my decision," I said.

"So okay then, if that's the way it's gotta be," Max said. "Good-by and good luck to you." He stood and started to move away, then turned back and, with exceptional tenderness, caressed Joleen's cheek. I stood at once in preparation for a confrontation, but Joleen showed no reaction to his uninvited gesture, nor did she give any sign that she required my intervention, and a short while later, Max desisted in his attentions to her, and once again made as if to leave. He turned back a second time, however, pivoting sharply on one foot and shooting a swift right toward my chin.

I stopped it with my own right hand and retained his hand in mine.

"You're quick all right," he said when I released his hand. I sat, and he sat down between us. "I see how you earned your nickname. But listen to this: here's a new one I just heard—'Confucious say that man who fish in other man's well often catch crabs.' Get it?"

Neither Joleen nor I laughed. Max punched me on the shoulder. "I got more where that came from," he said.

"We were enjoying a private dinner," Joleen said.

Max lifted Joleen's left hand, upon the third finger of which she wore the wedding band we had purchased at an F. W. Woolworth Five and Dime. We had taken to this ruse because we found that when we were in public establishments, men, seeing the ring, were less likely to make unwelcome advances upon her person than if we identified ourselves as brother and sister. This deception, I note, is the opposite of one the patriarch Abraham used when he believed himself and his wife Sarah to be in hostile territory: to ingratiate himself with those of whom he was wary, he declared that Sarah was his sister.

"Well, I ain't married yet, though I got women banging on my door all hours of the night and day," Max said. "And I ain't against hooking up with a good lady some day and making a few good-looking baby Baers too, but here's the thing of it: Watching from the bar, I said to myself, now there's a pair of gorgeous kids sweet on each other the way I'd like to have somebody sweet on me. And vice versa. But now that I know what's up, I gotta say that you two sure make marriage look like a swell thing."

"It has been that until your untimely arrival," Joleen said.

"So here's another one," he said. "'Confucious say that wife who put husband in doghouse soon find him in cathouse.'"

"Your vulgarity is exceeded only by your rudeness," Joleen said.

"True, true," Max said. "Sometimes, like now, I try too hard, and you know why?"

"No," Joleen said, "but I'm certain you will tell us."

"Because I want everyone to like me," Max said. "*Everyone!* Crazy, right? It's my Achilles' heel, for sure, except when I'm in the ring. The other guy may be the nicest guy in the world, but once the fight starts, we don't know each other. Once that bell goes ding-dong, all I care about is him feeling the power I got here."

Saying this, he made a fist, offered it to Joleen, and opened it slowly. "Okay," he said, letting out a long breath. "I apologize. I'm butting in where I ain't been invited, but when I saw you two looking into each other's eyes the way you do—and both of you so goddamned beautiful!—I never seen a couple, black, brown, white, or yellow, as beautiful as you, and I just wanted . . ."

He turned away. "You wanted what?" Joleen asked.

"I just wanted to be near you, is all," he said. "I wanted to drink in some of what you give off that makes you so beautiful."

"That's all?"

"I wanted to touch you," he said.

"Yes," Joleen said. "And—?"

"And I had to come over and maybe get a chance to feel your skin against mine, maybe just in my fingers—"

"Please, then," Joleen said, and she set her hand upon the table, close to where Max's hands were resting. Max hesitated, his eyes those of a child seeking permission. I showed nothing.

Max chewed on his lower lip, looked at Joleen's hand and, very gently, placed his right hand on top of hers.

A moment later I let my hand rest on top of his.

He spoke to me: "When I got closer and saw your hands—kind of freakish, a guy your size, you don't mind my saying so—I guessed who you were right off, so I just kept on coming." He rubbed a finger along the curve of Joleen's wedding band. "And hey, maybe *this* is the ring for me—not that other one, where people get hurt, though I guess married people can hurt each other too."

Joleen stared at me, nodded slightly, and I discerned her meaning.

"Perhaps I can spar with you on occasion," I said to Max. "Given your reputation for reckless power, however, I will insist that we use twelve ounce gloves and wear headgear."

"You got a deal, " Max said, leaning forward. "But now I got an even better one. My family, we moved out to Livermore where we got a ranch—cattle, hogs, sheep, and stuff—and we could use some help. We call our place Twin Oaks Ranch, and we'd pay okay, you'd get room and board for free, the country air ain't bad—free too— and we could get to know each other and become friends."

"I intend to become a schoolteacher," Joleen said. "To that end, I am preparing for the licensing examinations here in San Francisco."

"And I am working toward my high school diploma," I said.

"Like my old man says—he's part Jew, you know—an education, that's something nobody can take away from you, and I agree, dumb as I am," Max said. "But out at Twin Oaks, you'd catch plenty of time to study, and maybe, with your smarts, you could put some learning into my kid sister and my brothers. We'd pay for that. I got two brothers, both younger than me—Buddy, who's a monster, bigger than me though he can't punch worth dick—and Augie, who's a butcher like the old man. We adopted him, see—he's Portuguese—and he's got even less between the ears than I do and could use some civilizing, so what do you say?"

"I say that you will need to spell out the terms in specific detail, for how and why are we to depend upon your word when we have known you for but a few minutes?" Joleen said. "Nor have you conferred with your family about what you propose. How then do you—?"

"How?" he interrupted. "*How?!* Because I *like* you! Because my family loves me and I'm their best hope and shining star, see, and the three of us together having good times—that's something I feel the way you feel blood pumping through your heart ready to explode to kingdom come, and when I feel it like this, I believe in it, and do you know why?"

"Pray tell us," Joleen said.

"Because I've got a million dollar body and a ten cent brain," he said, "but I'm gonna be heavyweight champion of the whole goddamned world! Me—Maximilian Adelbert Baer!"

Then he ordered another bottle of champagne and began telling us about his life before coming to California—about living in Nebraska, Colorado, and New Mexico, where his father had worked as a butcher, mostly in meat packing plants, and how, for the first time, in California, his family had been able to purchase their own ranch. That, he explained—the ranching and butchering—was where his power came from: building himself up lifting hogs, sledgehammering cows and fence posts, and hauling meat carcasses.

He talked on and on while we ate—our entrées had arrived— then gave us a huge grin, winked, closed his eyes, and let his head bump down onto the table. I put a finger to his neck. His pulse was slow and strong. Joleen took my hand in one of hers—the hand that had touched Max—after which, with her free hand, she began caressing his forehead in the tender way he had caressed her cheek.

It seemed magical—"Kismet" for sure, Joleen whispered—that on her twenty-first birthday we had met this remarkable man—the most gorgeous man she had ever known, she said, and a man through whose good offices we would soon begin what was certain to be a great, new adventure. I agreed, and reminded her that when we had passed through the village of Kismet, California, on our way to San Francisco, I had said that not only were we passing through Kismet but that in our new life Kismet would soon be passing through us.

On fire with expectation, Joleen and I ate, drank champagne, and exchanged kisses and, as Joleen sometimes did when we were aglow from our private pleasures, she began reciting from The Song of Solomon about how she was black but comely, and how my kisses were better than wine. I responded with words I had long before set to heart: "'How fair is thy love, my sister, my spouse!'" I said, "'How much better is thy love than wine! and the smell of thine ointments than all spices!'"

When all but a few patrons were left in the restaurant and, our plates cleared, we were drinking coffee, Max suddenly sat up, took the coffee cup from my hands, drank what was left, then set it down and lifted my water glass high in the air. I thought he was going to propose a toast, but instead he turned the glass upside down, letting the water spill onto his head, after which he shook himself from side to side the way a puppy does when it emerges from a lake.

He moved closer to Joleen. "I could fall in love with you in a split second if you weren't married," he said.

"Why would my being married stop you?" Joleen asked.

"Because of him," he said, gesturing to me. "I respect him too much."

"I believe that I respect him at least as much as you do, for in truth, my friend, I know him far better than you or anyone else might ever know him."

"And so—?" Max asked.

"And so we are joined in our respect for him."

"That's all?"

Joleen gave us her most bewitching smile, pressed a finger against my mouth to keep me from speaking, and for an instant I thought she was going to tell him the truth—that she and I were brother and sister, and that therefore she was free to reciprocate his affection. From the high flush in her cheeks, I could see how powerfully drawn she was to this man whose black hair, broad forehead, high cheek-bones, and wide-set slanting eyes gave him the look of a man of Eurasian ancestry, and I sensed she could tell from my expression—I felt heat emanating from my own cheeks—that in this too we were joined.

I pressed my lips to her palm, and she took this kiss and gave it to Max, upon his mouth, and in that moment I feared that the role of marital partner that had been mine on this evening, as on a multitude of evenings before this, might be destined to remain mine alone. As if to confirm my surmise, Joleen closed her eyes and touched her lips to Max's cheek in what could only be called—how rich the irony, we would later agree—a sisterly manner.

" 'Rise up, my love, my fair one, and come away,' " she said.

"That's the Bible," Max said. "You can't fool me."

Joleen blew on his eyes, small puffs that caused him to blink rapidly. " 'I will arise now, and go about the city in the streets, and in the broad ways I will seek whom my soul loveth,' " she said.

"A ranch with rolling hills and clean meadows would be better than city streets, take my word for it," Max said, and pointed a finger at me. "And that's Bible stuff again, right?"

"Correct," I said.

"Your wife ain't some kind of religious nut, is she?" Max said. "Because if she is, the deal's off."

"I am a lover of poetry," Joleen said, and she kissed Max again.

Max blushed, and when he did, Joleen laughed, which caused him to move away from her, sliding along the table until he was sitting beside me.

"I don't want to do anything to get you riled," he said,

"especially given how deep in the tank I am and how quick you are with those hands of yours. I'd be no match for you tonight, and I ain't too proud to say so, but here's the question: Do you two really like me, or am I totally bongo-bongo, or hey!—are you like people I know, from back when Dempsey and Tunney were king and queen of the hill, who believe in that free love stuff?"

"I have no idea what you are talking about," Joleen said, and she moved closer to him, looping her slender arm across *his* back so that her fingers could play a soft rat-a-tat-tat upon the outer edge of *my* shoulder. "But I suggest that instead of making inquiries, you act with courage. *Courage, mon ami bien aimé! Courage!*"

"That's French," Max said. "You can't fool me. I know French when I hear it."

Joleen flicked his ear with her tongue. "*Courage!*" she whispered. And then: "'As the lily among thorns, so is my love among the daughters.' Are you a thorn, Max Baer? Pray tell us. Are you a thorn in our garden?"

"Well, I sure ain't a lily!" he said and, roaring with laughter, he let his hand fall upon my lap. I did not remove it, and I knew that by my decision to *not* act—to *not* remove his hand—I had lost what was perhaps the last opportunity I would have to inform him that Joleen and I were not husband and wife, and—the ironies, though obvious, were too knotted to disentangle in a moment wherein the speed of what was happening and the dizzied slowness of my thoughts contrasted so starkly—it might also be possible—this thought formed more in retrospect than in the moment—that Joleen and I might never again in this life be fully intimate with one another.

My sad presentiments—what I came to think of as my intimations of intimacy's absence—proved true, although the probable permanence of my loss did not come home to me until ten months later, following upon Max's bout with Frankie Campbell, a bout that was to secure Max's reputation both as a legitimate contender for the heavyweight championship of the world, and as a ruthless killer. By this time, Joleen and I had been living on the Baer family ranch for more than half a year, where, known as husband and wife, we were employed as domestics. From time to time I also worked with Max as a sparring partner in a makeshift ring he and his brother Buddy had set up near the barn where the hogs were maintained. In the ten-month period following our meeting at Perfidie, Max had fought fifteen bouts, winning ten by knockout and two on points, his three losses resulting from what seemed to have been agreed-upon setups arranged by interested parties: one a loss on points, the other two on disqualifications for not heeding with sufficient dispatch the referees' commands to take himself to a neutral corner. In four of these fifteen fights I attended to him in his corner as one of his handlers.

For her part, Joleen took to tutoring Max's sister and his two brothers several afternoons a week, which sessions I attended in order to improve my abilities to express myself in writing and in speech. What I desired was to become adept at articulating with precision what it was I was thinking and feeling so that I might relieve the rage, guilt, and melancholy that, by turns, had begun threatening, with increasing frequency and intensity, to overwhelm me. If I could know what my truest feelings were—if I could *name* them!—I might, I believed, no matter how painful or humiliating they were, deprive them of their power over me.

During these months, and until the birth of our son, Horace Jr., Joleen and I became increasingly practiced at allusive ways of talking about those matters we had relished talking about before we met Max. Until that evening at Perfidie, we had, as I recall now, felt little embarrassment about what we did, about talking about what we did, or about asking particular favors of the other we imagined might increase the wonders we experienced in our intimate moments. Now, however, our physical intimacies retreating further into the past, we no longer talked about them except in the most arch and circumlocutory ways.

"We are, it would seem, become handmaidens and handlers to butchers," Joleen would say in one of her familiar tropes, "and the emphasis on the syllable 'hand,' my long-fingered companion, can not, after all, be gainsayed."

"After all what?" I would reply.

"You are correct," she would say, "and that, I respectfully submit, is the strange beauty of it."

"Of what?" I would say.

"Yes," she would say then. "You are doubtless correct in your affirmation."

After which, in our cottage, or in the kitchen or laundry of the Baer family home, she would announce that there were noble works still to be accomplished before the sun set, and saying this, she would wish me a good day or a good evening, and take her leave, in this way putting an end to the possibility of talk concerning those matters we had become accustomed to not talking about.

Like our great grandparents on our father's side, who, in southeast Louisiana, not far from what is now the town of Burgess Castle, had been house servants to plantation owners (thus, our ability to remain together as family), we too were become house servants, and with privileges, Joleen would remark bitterly, not unlike those of our forbears. But beyond such "privileges," she had learned from stories passed down to our mother from *her* mother—privileges that, then as now, were referred to under the rubric of *droit du seigneur*—there had been one benefit that was a rarity among our people of that antebellum time: literacy.

In Louisiana in the early and mid-nineteenth century, it had been illegal for a master or mistress to teach a slave to read or to write, and the fact that the mistress of the plantation where our great grandparents had labored—a middle-sized sugarcane enterprise without a grand mansion like those portrayed in popular fiction and film—had defied the law, for reasons unexplained, loomed large in our family's history, and doubtless contributed to our family's love of the written and spoken word, to our willingness to express respect and affection for white people, and to trust in the possibility of their fairness and generosity. "It takes a rich cotton planter to make a poor sugar planter," I recall my father saying, words he believed could apply with accuracy to a multitude of situations.

The notion of Max Baer as a *seigneur*, however, Joleen would state—and invariably in a voice laced in equal parts with amusement and bitterness—did strain the limits of one's imagination, in addition to which neither of us was foolish enough to believe what Max wished us to believe: that Joleen and I had freely *chosen* the life that was ours.

"Still, it is wonderful to live in an illusion when the illusion is laden with so many palpable luxuries," Joleen would say. "Don't you agree?"

"Yes," I would reply, "for by so believing, we avoid responsibility for the choices we have actually made."

"*Touché, mon frère,*" she would reply.

As for Max, although he wanted us to believe we were loyal to him because we had *chosen* to do so—"*I know you love me as much as I love you!*" he would say—he was never a man to put much stock in, or submit to, dreams or illusions. With the exception of the infrequent times when, as on the night we first met, he drank to excess, he took pride in never euphemizing unpleasant realities, and this was especially true in his attitude toward the craft of boxing.

Max was famous for his lackadaisical training regimen, even when he was in the final days of workouts for an upcoming fight. No matter the quality of the opponent, after a day of rigorous training what he enjoyed most of all was going out on the town—womanizing, carousing, and then sleeping late in the mornings. "I love to fight and I love to knock guys out," he would say. "But there are lots of other things I love too, and sometimes those other things are the winners."

What he loved above all was having a good time. "That's the main thing, Horace," he would say, propped up on an elbow above me, or lying back on a pillow, smoking a cigar, "not to forget to have a good time, right? That's the main thing, far as I can tell. I mean, I can lie to others—the ladies especially when that makes sense—but I never lie to myself, and that makes the difference because that's just who I am. Me—Maximilian Adelbert Baer."

And Max had been blessed with such exceptional talent—power out of all proportion to his size, stamina that was not vitiated by the high life he favored, and defensive reflexes that kept his face free of welts and scars—that his ability to mix a demanding schedule of victorious fights and an equally demanding social life became the wonder of the boxing world.

On the night of August 25, 1930, however, when he fought against Frankie Campbell in a ring constructed above home plate in San Francisco's Recreation Park, a park built a year after the great earthquake and fire of 1907, and a park where the city's beloved baseball team, the San Francisco Seals, played, his ability to rejoice equally in his sport and his pastimes suffered a tragic setback. The fight against Campbell was for the unofficial title of Pacific Coast champion, and Campbell, whose real name was Camilli, and whose brother, Dolph Camilli, would in later years become a star first baseman for the Brooklyn Dodgers baseball team, was an excellent and up-and-coming boxer, admired for his superb footwork.

Well past midnight on the morning of the fight, Max came to our cottage. He reeked, as he often did at such times, of cologne, sweat, and cigars, but he seemed quite sober, and terribly upset. He sat on a wooden chair, his head in his hands, and told us that early in the evening he had learned that his trusted friend and trainer, Tillie "Kid" Herman, had decamped and was working with Campbell. Max was so distraught that he did not request any private time with either Joleen or myself. He also refrained on that evening, as he did through all our years together, from making any least suggestion that the three of us should engage in the kind of activity à trois that many men were believed, then as now, to value above others (although their preference, in my experience, was more often for two women than for two men), even though I believe Joleen and I would have granted him this wish had he indicated his desire for it. On this evening, however, he desired only consolation, and when the desire for consolation waned, vengeance. What he wanted was nothing less than to destroy Tillie "Kid" Herman. Herman, however, was not his opponent.

Campbell was, and that evening, in the second round of the bout, after Campbell had clipped Max a glancing blow on the chin, and Max had slipped to one knee, Campbell, assuming Max would stay down for a count of five or six, made the mistake of waving triumphantly to the crowd, which ignited the full fury of Max's rage. Rising swiftly from the canvas, Max flew at Campbell just as Campbell turned back from the crowd to the ring, and smashed a mighty roundhouse right to the side of Campbell's head that turned Campbell around in a full circle and sent him sprawling onto the canvas.

We later learned that between rounds Campbell told Herman,

"Something feels like it broke in my head," but that Herman paid no heed to this, and sent Campbell back into the ring for round three. Campbell seemed fine for the next two rounds, staying away from Max while scoring decisively with swift, sharp jabs. Before the fifth round, however, Herman began taunting Max, jeering at him and calling him a sheenie clown with the brain of an ox, and even before the bell rang for the fight to recommence, Max, eyes blazing, had kicked away his stool and water bucket, pushed me and his other handlers aside, stood, and, pounding his gloves one against the other, chest level, taken three steps forward. I was thrilled to see him like this, for I knew he felt most truly himself in these moments—lost in a reverie wherein his body and hands had a life of their own and he had no idea of what they were doing, and little memory afterwards of what they had done. Thrilled as I was when he was this way, though, I also feared for the other fighter who, in the most literal sense, I knew, would soon, his lights extinguished, not know or recall what had befallen him.

Max plowed forward like the ox Herman had said he was, and in a matter of seconds had Campbell against the ropes and was hammering him relentlessly, blow after thundering blow, as if Campbell's head were a speed bag. One of Campbell's eyes closed and swelled with such swiftness it seemed a hand grenade had been surgically inserted behind it. Herman might have thrown in the towel then, as a responsible trainer should have, but he chose not to. Nor did the referee or attending physician stop the fight as those in the crowd who were not screaming for blood were urging them to do. Only when Campbell's head clanged against one of the metal turnbuckles that connected the ropes to the ring posts, and it was clear that only the ropes and Max's repeated blows to Campbell's head—which had become a bloody, puffed pulp—were holding him up, did the referee step between the fighters. Had he not, Max, so enraged and inspired was he—so lost in the sheer, brute joy of smashing blow after blow at Campbell in a futile attempt to exact a vengeance that would never be his—that he might have gone on throwing punches forever.

When the referee stepped in, and Max stepped away, Campbell fell forward face first to the canvas and lay there unconscious while the referee counted him out, after which I rushed into the ring, turned Campbell over, lifted his head, placed a towel under it, and poured water onto his face. Campbell did not stir or open his eyes. We called for an ambulance, and while Campbell lay on the canvas, immobile, for half an hour—the ambulance became stuck in traffic, we were informed—boxing fans crowded into the ring to gawk at him, and neither police nor boxing officials did anything to clear the ring or to initiate other ways of removing Campbell from it. When at last an ambulance from St. Joseph's Hospital arrived, Max helped carry Campbell out on a stretcher. A few hours later we received a telephone call informing us that Campbell was near death.

At St. Joseph's, Max paced the hallway where Campbell's wife, Elsie, sat, and cradled her and Campbell's newborn son in her arms. Max offered his hand to Campbell's wife—offered to cut it off and give it to her—but she only pressed Max's hand between her own hands. "It's all right," she said. "It even might have been you, mightn't it?"

Frankie Campbell died at noon the next day, and when he did— we had stayed overnight in the hospital's waiting room in anticipation of the news—Max broke down and sobbed like a baby. For days, out at the ranch, he was inconsolable, and for years afterwards would wake from nightmares in which he relived those moments when the only thing he knew how to do—to be Max Baer—was to continue to rain down blows upon a strong man made increasingly helpless by these very blows. It was in the near aftermath of Campbell's death that Max came to accept and depend, almost desperately, upon the loving-kindness Joleen offered him, and in a way that made me realize again, more fully than I wanted to, that although her love for me would remain undiminished, her intimate affections might never again be mine.

Max was charged with manslaughter by the office of the San Francisco District Attorney, and a warrant for his arrest issued, to which he surrendered. He spent several hours behind bars at the Hall of Justice, but was released on bail in an amount that equaled his take for the fight. Although he was, a few months later, acquitted of charges, the State Boxing Commission banned him from any in-ring activity in California for a full year, a year during which Max fought six bouts out of state—he could not *not* fight—including three at Madison Square Garden, so swiftly was his reputation—and his value as a drawing card for having killed a man—on the rise. (He donated the purses from these fights to Frankie Campbell's family, and he did so without seeking publicity. In later years, again without publicity, he helped put three of Frankie Campbell's children through college at the University of Notre Dame.)

So distressed was he during this year, however, that he lost four of his half-dozen fights, and it was while I held him in my arms in the early morning following upon the third of these losses—to the Basque and European heavyweight champion Paolino Uzcudun, in a bout in Reno, Nevada, refereed by Jack Dempsey—that he asked if I would promise to do him the honor—"the honor, Horace, please" he kept repeating—to travel with him for *all* his fights, for he did not know how, during the hours and days between fights, he would survive without me.

But survive he did, and a month before the first anniversary of Campbell's death, Max's innate and unrestrained love of life, and of women, flourishing more with each passing day, prevailed, so that on July 8, 1931, after a headline-producing courtship, he married Dorothy Dunbar (thereby becoming the fifth of her seven husbands), and his love for Dorothy, and marriage to her, seemed to revive him. "I think I love being in love even more than I love knocking guys out," he said to me on his wedding day, and during his first year of marriage he won all ten of his fights. Although, following the wedding, he and Dorothy quickly began their dance of separating, having affairs with others, and reuniting, the marriage itself, which reinforced in him the belief that he was, despite Campbell's death, worthy of love, seemed also to intensify and increase his attentions to me and to Joleen.

It was ever thus, and would remain so for as long as we were with him, we came to realize: the more he loved others, the more he loved us. "The way I see it," he said in our hotel room after he had, in Oakland, California, a day before the New Year of 1932, defeated the highly-ranked Italian Arthur De Kuh, "the more time I spend in bed with you—the better I am in the ring."

And a few months later, when we were staying at the Plaza Hotel in New York City, to which he had shipped ten trunks of clothes and thirty tailor-made suits, so devoted had he become to the night life of the city, and so pleased by the attention given him for his extravagant ways by the press, that he could declare, as if confiding a secret, that he agreed with the sportswriters that he had become, at twenty-one years old, in his own words, "as magnificent a piece of young American manhood you'd ever want to lay your hands on." It was not merely the natural endowments—his dark skin, deep-set eyes, curly black hair, chiseled chin, and broad shoulders that were his by birth, but something else—the fact that being in love, whether with Dorothy, Joleen, me, or others, had turned out, he said, to be the same as training for a fight: the secret of success lay in repetitions. That was why things were always so good with Dorothy, even when she continued—as she had before she divorced the Span-ish diplomat Jaime De Gerson y Baretto to marry Max—to toy with him.

"She toys with me—sure," he said. "But that's okay because I *am* a toy! And thank the good lord I am, because I love to be played with as much as I love to play, and I don't have to prove that to you, I bet."

So he and Dorothy fought, split up, took on lovers, and got back together, and the more they carried on in this manner, the happier he became, and the better he fought. "What I figured out," he said to me on the night before his second fight with Ernie Schaaf, on the last day of August 1932 (Schaaf had beaten him badly—perhaps his worst loss ever—twenty months before, in his first bout following on Campbell's death), "is that when I'm in love it's like when I'm in the ring, because that's when time goes whiz-bang and I can't even tell where my body begins and my mind ends, and vice versa, though with the peanut-sized brain I got, maybe *nobody'd* be able to tell."

What I thought but did not say in response to such remarks was that when it came to love, what concerned me first, last, and always, was the fate of the woman he claimed to love above all others. For what was Joleen to do with herself—with her life!—during the many months Max and I were away, especially since, on the few oc-casions we did return to Livermore—three in total that first year of his marriage—Dorothy accompanied us.

Only once, to my knowledge, were Max and Joleen able during that period to be alone together. On that day in mid-July, a month before his second fight with Schaaf, I had served breakfast to Doro-thy in the Baer home (Max had earlier announced he was going for a morning run with his brother Buddy), after which I had returned to our cottage in order to ready myself for a sparring session with him. To my surprise—for I did not expect he would chance being with Joleen while Dorothy was at the ranch—I found him sitting on our bed. Joleen stood by the window, her arms crossed above her breasts. Both she and Max were fully clothed, and neither of them was smiling.

"But you *are* the best," he was saying as I entered our cottage. "Like I told you—you're my number one and only sweetheart."

"So are all the others," Joleen replied.

"But don't you know how true it is for me, like I always say—that the darker the cherry, the sweeter the meat?" he said.

"As far as I can tell," Joleen said, "the sweetest meat is whatever's in your mouth."

"Well, maybe," Max said. "It's true I got a huge appetite."

"Then you should go and feed it," she said, and opened the door to indicate that it was time for him to leave. "My husband and I are entitled to our privacy."

And saying this, she turned away from him and kissed me passionately, although, my back to him, I could not tell if Max took notice. I extricated myself from Joleen's embrace as quickly as I could, and by the time I did, he was gone.

Pushing me away angrily, Joleen swiped at her mouth with the back of her hand. " 'Vengeance is mine, saith the Lord,' " she declared. "And though it may be so, let me tell you this, my brother— I want *my* share too."

"You are upset," I said.

"How can you tell?"

"You surely have reason for your bitterness, and—" I began, but she cut me off by grabbing me by the throat.

"Are you not curious as to how I will have my share of vengeance?" she asked.

"Pray tell me," I said.

"*Pray tell me?!*" she said. " 'Pray tell me,' did he say? Oh you may mock me, brother dear, but I *will* have vengeance—a great, endur-ing vengeance that will dwarf all the minor perturbations of this life. Do not doubt me, thee of meager faith. And how? *How?* Tell me, my love. How will I have *my* portion?"

Aware that nothing I could do or say would temper her rage, I remained silent.

"A tongue hath he, yet he speaks not," she said, and gripped my throat more forcefully. "*How?* How long, oh Lord, I must wonder, can this fool—this coward I have called my dearest friend and soul mate—keep from inquiring as to *how* I will have my share in the time to come?"

Blood pulsing with increasing force behind my eyes, I considered prying her thumbs upwards with force—of breaking one of them if need be, or of visiting a blow upon her cheek with the back of my hand that would have cracked bone there—yet I was also able in the moment to find a place within me that said: Go slow, Horace. Go slow, my friend, for you dare not add physical pain to the distress of her soul. Be kind if you can. Be kind.

As if she discerned my thoughts at the very moment they were making themselves known to me, she loosened her hold upon my throat.

I sucked in quick, shallow breaths of air, and then: "How?" I asked. "How will you have your vengeance?"

"Thank you for asking," she replied. "How? Why, by having his child—that is how. I will have Max Baer's child. Since I can-not . . . since we can never . . ."

That was when something inside her, like the branch of a sap-ling, seemed to snap in two. She let go of me, sat on our bed, slumped forward, and wept. I was not surprised by what she had said, or by what she had begun to say, for we had decided long be-fore, and had ever taken necessary precautions, to make certain our love would not bring a new life into this world. So I sat beside her, took her hand in mine, and said that given our place in Max's life—in the world!—we needed, now more than ever, to exercise caution. We needed not to act from a raw desire for vengeance, as urgent as that desire might be.

Through her tears, Joleen asked what if not raw desire had *our* life together been about. Until this moment, she had believed that no matter how dark the way in this life might be, she would always be able to count on me. But now . . .

"But now, more than ever, you can," I said softly. "For I am acting out of a desire beyond the desire that has made us one with the other. I am acting out of a desire to protect you."

"From *him*?" she said. "Do not talk nonsense to me. He is a mere child. Protect me from *him*?!"

"Protect you from yourself," I said.

"*I will have Max Baer's child!*" she declared again and, wiping away her tears, she stood and went to the door. "And now, my husband, there are chores that await, and I must be gone. Do you object?"

"I love you more than life," I said. "I always will."

"Do not utter banal nonsense in my presence," she said. "And do not underestimate me. I want vengeance, yes, but knowing me—*loving* me, as you would have it, and are not, in the biblical sense, knowing and loving one and the same?—you should also *know* that there is nothing in the smallest digit of my smallest finger or toe that is, or ever has been, self-destructive. During your peregrinations with our lord and master, I have had more than ample time for reflection, and before this day decided that of course I will *not* have his child—that *we* will not have his child . . . not, that is, until he has had a child by another, preferably a *white* woman to whom he is married. For that is the path of wisdom and safety."

"In this I do not think you should count upon having Dorothy serve as your accomplice," I said.

"For the honor of bearing Max Baer's child, there will be no shortage of candidates," she said. "*You* can count on that. Do not fret more than is necessary, though, for as enraged as I can be, I can also, as you know better than anyone, be ruthlessly patient." She came near to me again, breathing her words into my ear: "I can await the day when I will whisper to him as I now do to you: 'O that thou wert as my brother, that sucked the breasts of my mother!' "

" 'Jealousy can be as cruel as the grave,' " I said, speaking words that followed on those in the verse from which she had quoted. " 'The coals thereof are coals of a fire which hath a most vehement flame.' "

"Ah—but 'love is as strong as death,' " she responded, reciting a line I had, as she of course knew, taken care to omit. Her mouth on my cheek, her teeth scraping at the corner of *my* mouth, I knew well the words she would speak next. " 'When I should find thee without, I would kiss thee—for yea, I should not be despised.' "

Then, one hand holding fast to the back of my neck, she kissed me full on the mouth.

On the eve of Max's second bout with Schaaf, I recalled this moment, and doing so made me realize yet again that what drove Max above all—what enabled him to be the invincible fighter he could often be—were not merely his athletic gifts or his power, but, as with Joleen, the ferocity of his will: the desire, when roused, to triumph over and wreak vengeance upon anyone and everyone who had humbled him, or who threatened to humble him, so that he would not ever in the eyes of others, or, more tellingly, his own, be despised.

Twenty months earlier, Schaaf had humbled Max. An

all-services champion while serving in the navy, Schaaf was more a boxer than a puncher, but on that night, with Dorothy (still married to De Gerson y Baretto) at ringside, Schaaf had mauled Max. Max prided himself on never having been seriously hurt in a fight, and in the dressing room before the fight, in front of an entourage of reporters who doted on him for his style and flash, he had put on his usual show of good-humored nonsense, delighting reporters on that occasion—a first—by ramming into a radiator headfirst to demonstrate the thickness of his skull.

Once the fight began, however, Schaaf made an increasingly confused Max chase him around the ring (Schaaf was one of the few left-handed boxers Max had hitherto faced), stopping only to sting Max with quick, telling right jabs. By the eighth round, Max's beautiful face was unrecognizable, and I found myself pleading with him to let me throw in the towel. But Max would have none of it and, remarkably, remained game for the full ten rounds, thereby gaining the respect of many who doubted his courage and stamina simply by being in an upright position when the referee held up Schaaf's right hand to award him the victory.

This time, however, before a large crowd at Chicago Stadium, with a string of ten consecutive victories under his belt, and with Dorothy, his wife of seven weeks, at ringside, Max was ready. From the opening bell, he went after Schaaf, pounding him at will while at the same time withholding the ultimate blow in the way a bullfighter weakens a bull with many thrusts of his sword so that one final thrust above the eyes will bring the bull to its knees. After battering Schaaf without mercy for nine rounds, Max waited until there were but two seconds left in the tenth and final round before unleashing his most vicious punch, a brutal right chop to the head that floored Schaaf for the first time that night, and left him, like Campbell, unconscious.

Max blew Dorothy a kiss and strutted around the ring, yet even while the crowd cheered, and while Schaaf's seconds dragged him to his corner and worked to restore him to his senses (it would be an exact three minutes, the length of a round, before Schaaf opened his eyes), Max, clinging to me, whispered his fear.

"Did I hurt him the way I hurt Campbell?" he asked. "Tell me, Horace. Tell me, please. Tell me I didn't, okay? I was just toying with him, really. He's an okay fighter, but I carried him tonight, Horace. I didn't hurt him bad, did I? I could have done him in early, but . . ."

"You fought a good fight," I said. "You were powerful yet merciful."

As if I had thrust a knife into his belly, Max pulled away. "Don't you *lie* to me, Horace," he said. "Don't you ever *dare* lie to me, do you hear? Do you *hear*? I ain't the fool you or anyone else takes me for."

Then he turned away and, after blowing kisses to the crowd, went to Schaaf's corner, embraced him, and told him he was the best fighter he had ever faced.

A month later, in the same stadium, Max easily defeated Tuffy Griffiths, a fighter who had once won fifty consecutive bouts before being knocked out by the future champion James Braddock, and the newspapers confirmed our hope: that Max would soon be given a shot at the title. Before this could happen, however, we returned to New York City's Madison Square Garden to watch Schaaf fight Primo Carnera, who was first in line, ahead of Max, for a challenge to the reigning champion, Jack Sharkey.

Schaaf was as game against Carnera as Max had been in his first fight against Schaaf, but he was clearly not the fighter he had been before his bout against Max. In the eleventh round, Carnera landed a light blow to Schaaf's chin that, surprisingly, caused Schaaf to go limp and drop to the canvas, where he lay, unmoving.

He never woke up, and when he died two days later, Max agreed with what the boxing world quickly concluded: that it was not Carnera's blow that had killed Schaaf, but the savage beating, six months earlier, Max had inflicted upon him. Max brooded on this—on the labels of "killer" and "butcher" that now attached to his name virtually every time it appeared in print—even while his will to be champion became more inflamed. Nor did he shy away from keeping himself in the public eye. Rather the opposite. So that, as he prepared for what would be the major fight of his life thus far, against Max Schmeling at the Yankee Stadium in New York City, he courted journalists as never before—taking me, and his trainer, Mike Cantwell, and his publicist, Sam Taub, with him on endless rounds of newspaper offices, where he entertained reporters with antics that included using Taub for a punching bag and then jamming him into a wastebasket. And two weeks before the bout, he told me, in confidence, of his decision to enter the ring at the Yankee Stadium with a large Star of David emblazoned on the right leg of his boxing trunks, thereby declaring to the world that he was a Jew who was ready to stand up to a German known to be the favorite of the German people's new leader, Adolf Hitler. "You just watch and see, Horace—this is gonna make me immortal in the eyes of the whole goddamned world!"

Although Max was only one-quarter Jewish—his father's father was Jewish, which made him even less Jewish than former champion Jack Dempsey, whose paternal grandmother was Jewish—Max gloried in the way the press took up the story, especially given news arriving from Europe about the oppressive measures the Third Reich was inflicting upon Jews.

"Hey," he told reporters in the dressing room before the fight when one of them questioned how Jewish he was, "seems like over there, whether you're part-Jew or all-Jew, you pay the same price, so you can bet your mother's whiskers I'm gonna show this Kraut that we Jews know how to take care of ourselves."

And when on the night of June 8, 1933, with Jack Dempsey, one of the bout's promoters, at his side, Max came out of the runway and onto the long, open aisle that led to the ring, some 60,000 people roared their approval. "See what I mean, Horace?" he said to me while waving to the crowd. "My people are here the same as yours would be if you were in the ring against one of those Great White Hope guys the way Jack Johnson was. This city's full of Jews, and they're gonna love me even more after I knock the living daylights out of Hitler's pillow-boy."

Schmeling, who had briefly been world heavyweight champion after defeating Sharkey, and before losing the title to him in a return match, was a fighter who, unlike Max, trained with thoroughgoing efficiency, and did not party at night. The bookmakers had established him as a four-to-one favorite, and these odds served only to inspire Max. "Jews have always been the scapegoats and underdogs," he told reporters when they asked how he felt about the supposed smart money going against him. "It's why we learned to fight harder—the more people try to keep us down, see, the more we rise up and conquer. Just like we did against that Pharaoh guy."

Max started out on fire—"a human tornado," the *New York Times* would call him the next day—but then, as often happened, once he demonstrated he could dominate his opponent, he seemed to become bored, and to merely go through the motions. Before the tenth and last round, however, Dempsey and Cantwell screamed at him that if he didn't wake up—for Schmeling, plodding doggedly ahead, was landing short punches that had clearly put him ahead on points—he would lose the fight.

"Okay then," Max said, and he came roaring out of the corner at the start of the tenth round, going at Schmeling as if it were the fight's opening round. Within seconds, he had landed a huge right to Schmeling's jaw that sent the German to the canvas. Schmeling rose at the count of nine, but Max was on top of him with a furious barrage of lefts and rights that had Schmeling stumbling around the ring until Max, holding him upright on the ropes with his left hand, unleashed another devastating right—"This one's for Hitler!" he announced, loud enough for those in the front rows to hear—that made Schmeling stagger helplessly in retreat, as if drunk, and that left the referee no alternative but to stop the fight and declare Max the winner by a technical knockout.

Max was ecstatic afterwards, proclaiming to reporters that he would soon become the heavyweight champion of the world, and declaring to me, before he left the stadium to go out on the town with June Knight, his newest sweetheart—a twenty-year old movie star and *Ziegfeld Follies* headliner—that what he proved in the ring was that he had his people just like I had mine.

"What I showed out there tonight, Horace, is that we gotta take care of each other the way we been doing," he said, "because the rest of the world's always ready and waiting to do us in. Kikes and niggers—we gotta stick together, ain't I right?"

"Perhaps," I said. "But you are only a kike if you choose to call yourself one. Your people possess a long and rich history, and it behooves you not to make of this history a joke, but to cherish it even as Joleen and I, who are not of your Mosaic persuasion, have learned to do."

"Hey," he said, and he wrapped his arms around me and gave me a big, sloppy kiss on the cheek. "Don't you know how to tell it, Horace, and with words to burn. And ain't you the smartest nigger anyone ever knew—this Jewboy first of all!"

I pressed the palm of my hand against his chest and pushed him away—we were in the corridor outside the dressing room, and could hear the riotous chanting of fans who waited on the other side of the exit door—and when I did, he grabbed my hand in his own so that for a moment I thought he would try to crush it. Instead, he took it to his chest and pressed it there.

"Shit, Horace," he said, his eyes moist. "I'm sorry, okay? I didn't mean nothing—you know that, don't you? I got nothing for you and your wife but all the love and respect I ever had for anyone. Just ask June here, about how I been talking about you two, and how smart you are and what I been learning from you."

"He really loves you like he says," June said, and gave me a smile such as the one that must have won the heart of Mister Ziegfeld. "So come on out and play with us tonight. Our Mister Max knows how to have a good time better than anyone. Come on out and play with us tonight, pretty please?"

2   Champion of the World

Go forth, O ye daughters of Zion, and
behold king Solomon with the crown
wherewith his mother crowned him in the
day of his espousals, and in the day of the
gladness of his heart. (3:11)

In the year that followed on Max's victory over Schmeling—until he fought and defeated Primo Carnera for the heavyweight championship of the world—Max continued to excel at what he loved most: having a good time. It was a year during which we spent most of our time in New York and Los Angeles (where Max purchased a home overlooking the Pacific Ocean), and during which he divorced Dorothy, had highly publicized romances with several movie stars, and starred in his first movie, playing opposite Myrna Loy in *The Prizefighter and the Lady*.

Max delighted in the praise he received from critics for his role in *The Prizefighter and the Lady*, in the women who pursued him because of it (Jean Harlow, relentlessly aggressive, would show up at our home uninvited on evenings when she knew Max was entertaining other women), and, especially, in the news that Joseph Goebbels, Hitler's Minister of Propaganda and Entertainment, had banned it in Germany. That, he declared, was the kind of fame you couldn't buy.

It was also a year during which Joleen went through an unexpected and alarming transformation. This was apparent at once when, five months after the premiere of *The Prizefighter and the Lady*, Max and I returned to Livermore and, entering the cottage Joleen and I shared (this was our first visit home since Max's triumph over Schmeling), we found Joleen sitting cross-legged on the floor, playing with two cloth dolls. The dolls, which Joleen and I had taken with us when we left Texas, had belonged to our mother, and to her mother before that. Known as pickaninny dolls—a locution that had no derogatory association at that time, being merely a literal reference to Negro children, and deriving from a mixture of Portuguese (*pequenino*), and Creole (*pinkin ningre*)—they had lost their original button eyes, most of their looped yarn hair, and the stitchings of their embroidered mouths, so that they were by now of indecipherable age or gender.

Joleen showed neither surprise nor happiness—no reaction at all, in fact—at our unannounced arrival. She continued to play with the dolls as if we were not there—talking to them, placing them in a wooden vegetable crate, covering them with a piece of frayed red-checkered fabric, kissing them, and wishing them pleasant dreams.

"My ghosts," she said to Max. And then: "Has my husband told you about my dead brother?"

My heart stopped briefly, and returned with such a strong thump-thump that I thought Max would hear it. His eyes fixed on Joleen, however, he paid me no attention.

"Hey—" he said to her, his arms spread wide, "ain't you got some welcome-home hugs and kisses for us long-lost guys?"

Joleen took her Bible from the top of a bookcase that was set at right angles, in an L-shape, against the footboard of our bed and an adjacent wall. "You have not answered my question," she said. She sat, and opened her Bible. "When you have replied to my question, I will reply to yours."

"Okay," Max said. "Sure. So the answer's no—he never said nothing about any brother."

"That is a shameful but correctable omission," Joleen said.

"Glad to hear it," Max said. "So now that I answered your question like you asked, how about those hugs and kisses?"

"Of course," Joleen said, and she rose and, as if she herself had become a cloth doll, embraced each of us in a limp, perfunctory manner.

"Since my husband has been dilatory in telling you of this chapter in our lives—nor, I confess, have I been as forthcoming as I might have been—I will tell it to you," she said. "But be forewarned: it is not a tale that will inspire joy or hope, and it is one that will surely bring me down with gray hairs to the grave."

Max turned to me. "Do you know what the hell's going on here, Horace?" he asked. "I can understand your wife being pissed at us for being away so long, and maybe it was bad manners to bust in here first thing, but that was just my way of showing how *much* I missed you, see, and—"

"You are a child, Max Baer," Joleen said. "And a fool, which is doubtless why so many adore you, though I do not, for such reasons, count myself among them."

"Ah come on," Max said. "You know how you feel about me, so why don't you sweeten up and we'll make amends, okay? Amends—that's the right word, ain't it? I mean, you can punish me later any way you want for being gone so long—only don't be getting sore at Horace. He ain't to blame for nothing, and hey—to show how much I been thinking about you, I brought you some stuff from New York you're gonna love."

"Do you want to hear about my brother?" Joleen asked.

"You know it," Max said. "Only I ain't spent time with my own family yet, and *my* brother Buddy's hungry for getting me in the ring so we can bang each other around. But I'll be back after, and with the surprises I brought for you, okay?"

"I take no pleasure from material gifts," Joleen said. "Be assured, however, that despite my subdued manner, I do retain considerable affection for you, as I do for my husband. Before the enormity of my brother's death, however, and my memory of it, the memories of our times together—you and me, sir—do, necessarily, grow small."

"I get what you're telling me," Max said. "Sure. So how about I give you two lovebirds some private time together and come back after dinner, and you tell me your story then. I'd be glad to hear it. Really."

"You say that you will be glad to hear it—true in prospect, yes, though in the hearing of it, I expect, no," she said, and then, more softly: " 'By night on my bed I sought him whom my soul loveth: I sought him, but I found him not.' "

"But we're *here* now!" Max said. "So you don't got to worry no more. Like they say—lost and found, and found is better than lost, right?"

"Perhaps," Joleen said. "But you must also distinguish between 'lost' and 'loss,' and it is the latter that troubles my days of late, though it need not trouble yours. So take your leave of me to be with those others you love, and whether your word proves true or not—whether you return or wander away again—know this: I will have vengeance, Max Baer."

"Oh sure," Max said. "I can understand that."

Joleen smiled for the first time since our arrival. "You can understand what?"

"About me coming and going so much—more going than coming, that's for sure."

"I do not think you heard my words," Joleen said, and she repeated them in the same toneless manner as before: "I will have vengeance, Max Baer."

"Against who?" Max asked.

"Against *whom*," Joleen said, correcting him.

"Whom—sure," Max said. "And I don't envy whoever—whomever?—it is you got a grudge against, because I know you, Joleen, and I can tell just how royally pissed off you are from how goddamned calm you're being. But you know what? Inside you, sweetheart, you seethe with rage the way I do, and the same goes for Silent Sam here—it's why we click so good, the three of us. I figured that out a long time back—only the difference, see, is that when I'm pissed off, I don't know how to hide it because I don't *want* to hide it."

"Hide and seek?" Joleen asked.

"Oh yeah," Max said. "Hide and seek. Sure. I see what you mean. So like I said—I'll be back after supper."

It was dark when he returned to our cottage, and he came bearing gifts that he laid out upon our bed: silk scarves, small flasks of perfumes and ointments, a lacquered jewelry box containing a bracelet made of baroque pearls, a barrette delicately inlaid with mother-of-pearl, a pale pink diaphanous scarf embroidered with seed pearls, and a necklace of round, natural pearls, which were, Max said proudly, the most valuable pearls in the world. It was called a *princess*-length necklace, which, since she was his one and only princess, he declared, was the reason he'd bought it for her.

"And are you then my prince, Max Baer?" Joleen said as she removed the gifts from our bed and placed them in the crate with her dolls. "If so, you might consider that the prince of princes himself declared the kingdom of heaven—a place, I expect, none of *us* will ever know—to be itself a pearl of great worth."

"Sure, sure," Max said, grinning. "The prince of princes—I get it—but do you *like* what I got for you?"

"I am grateful for your kindness," Joleen said. "You are and ever have been a thoughtful man."

"Well yeah," Max said. "Only I don't want you to think I chose what I did because of what they cost. Like I always say: money's just money, and the easiest way to pay for things in this life is with money."

"How true," Joleen said. "Especially for those who *have* money."

"But I bet you're wondering why all the pearls, right?" Max said.

"No," Joleen said.

"Okay then," Max said. "So I'll tell you. It's because they come from the deep."

"And so—?"

"And so? And so they're like *you*, see—they come from a place that's so deep you can't figure out what's going on there. They grow at the bottom of the ocean—sure—we know *that*, but what I mean is they're deep because nobody understands how things so beautiful can grow in the dark from almost nothing, and get to be what they are."

"There is no mystery as to how pearls come into being," Joleen said.

"*That ain't what I mean!*" Max shouted. "That ain't what I

mean at all and you know it!" And then: "You're giving me a hard time just so you can rile me up, right? I say black and you say white, and I say hot and you say cold, and—sure—now that I'm back home there ain't *nothing* I can say or do that's gonna get you to agree with me on *anything,* is there?"

"I do not understand why you are upset with me," Joleen said. "I appreciate your gifts, and have shown my gratitude by making a home for them in a place that is dear to me, and where—"

"It's because *you're* such a goddamned mystery, don't you get it?" Max said. "*That's* why I got them for you. If I wanted to bring you baubles like I do for a lot of dames, I could've done that, but I *thought* about what to bring that would *mean something,* and here you go and crap all over them."

"Not at all, my friend," Joleen said. "I and my children will cherish them."

"Your *children*?!" Max asked, and he turned to me. "What the hell is she talking about? *What* children?"

"Her dolls," I said.

Max looked bewildered. "I also thought of how beautiful they would look against your skin," he said. "Because they're *like* you but they're *not* like you, see? They're beautiful, and there's nothing fake about them, and they come from a grain of sand the way you, me, and Horace come from something invisible you can't see with your naked eye."

"But it is not true that—" Joleen began.

"Don't you go cutting me off with your highfaluting crap," Max snapped. "I'm not some dunce the way you and everyone tries to make out, because sure I know about how things are born—pearls *or* people—but *knowing* how it happens don't take away from the *mystery* of it. It's still a mystery no matter how much we know. It's like . . . it's like . . ."

"It's like what, Max?" Joleen asked.

"I don't know," Max said. "It's like love, I guess—like falling in love."

"Yes," Joleen said.

"I said it," Max said. "I said the magic word. So *now* are you happy?"

"Does it matter?" Joleen asked.

"Sure it matters," Max said. "It's the most important thing there is, being happy and in love. What else is there?"

"Loss," Joleen said. "And there is also mystery, as you have suggested. Loss and mystery. There is the great unknown from which we come and to which we go, and there is all that we lose when we are between these worlds."

Max turned to me. "Do you understand her when she talks like this, Horace?" he asked.

"Sometimes," I said.

"Not me," Max said. "Seems like hide-and-seek to me, but without rules, if you get what I mean."

"I don't," I said.

"Good," Max said, and he whacked me on the shoulder. "So I guess that means *I'm* a mystery too, right?"

"You have always been a mystery to me, Max Baer," Joleen said.

"Ah," Max said, smiling. "And here I been thinking I had you fooled about me being the fool you been saying I am."

"You have always been a mystery to me, Max Baer," Joleen said again. "A *sweet* mystery despite your vocation—your penchant for inflicting violence upon others—though about that, as you will soon learn, I am no stranger, so please sit. Please sit, and I will tell you about my brother."

"Sure thing," Max said. "Only first—"

And before either Joleen or I could stay his hand, he had reached into the dolls' bed, taken out the necklace, and held it against Joleen's throat.

"Will you look at that!" he exclaimed. "Just *look* at that! I been thinking about how wonderful amazing it would look against your skin ever since I saw it in New York, and—"

Joleen seized Max's hand, wrested the necklace from it and, holding its clasp at one end, began whipping it against a wall—as if killing a snake—until the pearls sprung loose, sprayed into the air, and clattered to the floor.

"Holy shit," Max said.

"You did not ask my permission," Joleen said, and though her voice remained calm, in her eyes I saw a look that reminded me of nothing else but the look in Max's eyes when, without mercy, he would be pummeling an opponent to the canvas. "They were my pearls once they were given to me, were they not?"

Max stared at the back of his hand, now red with blood. Quickly, I wet a cloth and gave it to him, and he wiped the blood away, wrapped his hand in the cloth.

"Holy shit," he said again. "But they sure looked beautiful next to your skin—more beautiful than I imagined. And that's worth the world to me . . . but holy shit, Joleen . . ."

On my hands and knees, I began to gather the pearls.

Joleen went to our cupboard, took out a candle, lit it, and knelt at my side. "When we lose the most valuable objects in the world, we search for them with a candle that costs but a penny," she said. "My mother taught me that."

"You're *nuts*," Max said. "You're also a bitch, but that don't matter. I've known plenty of bitches in my time. You're mean too— but mostly you're a nut job. Totally bonkers, and maybe that's all there is to it, to what I could never figure out till now."

Joleen blew out the candle, stood, and, without acknowledging what Max said, she took his hand—the one she had scratched—in her own. He did not resist. She unwrapped the cloth, wiped away the blood, and then rewrapped his hand.

"I am a woman whose habits are such that you need not fear the loss of your much vaunted power," she said. "I will gather the pearls later on—they have no means of escape, after all—and I will restring them so that they will be as before. I trust that will make you happy. But now, my friend, please sit beside my husband and I will tell you about my brother."

Max sat on the bed next to me. Although I took comfort from the fact that Joleen had, several times, referred to me as her husband, I remained wary, and to comfort myself I reached for Max's hand, the one Joleen had scraped raw, and held it in mine, and when I did he gave me a smile so innocent it made me want to comfort *him*.

"I never was a child, really," Joleen began. "As I have told you before, I grew up on small farms owned by white people, mostly in southeast Louisiana, where my parents and older siblings worked as sharecroppers and domestics. I am not going to talk this evening of what our life was like back then, however, except to say it was not unlike that of other poor Negroes, nor was it unlike the lives of poor white families who lived nearby, though we had little commerce with them. In point of fact, I never talked with a white person until I had passed my ninth birthday.

"I will talk tonight of my brother James, whom I loved dearly, and of his death, and of how this led to my taking leave of my family, to my marriage to Horace, and to the honor that has become mine: of knowing you as my friend, Max Baer, of benefiting from the generosity of your heart, and of the honor of bearing my husband's good name, Littlejohn, so that living here as I do, under the protective love of two good men, no one who knew me, or of me, and of what occurred before and after my brother's death, will ever, should my good fortune hold, find me and punish me."

"Your husband's a good man," Max said, "and a fine boxer too. If he'd let me get him some bouts, he could clean up and rise almost as fast as me. But he's more stubborn than smart most days."

Max punched me in the shoulder with his free hand, and I didn't flinch.

"See that?" he said. "He can take a punch good as anyone, and—"

"Enough," Joleen said.

"Shh," Max said, a finger at his lips, his mouth close to my ear. "You got one hell of a wife, you know, even if she's bats some of the time, but let me tell you this too—when it comes to a wife who's beautiful and bats, I been there, my friend."

He started laughing, but stopped as soon as he became aware of the severe look Joleen was giving him.

"My brother James was older than I by two years," Joleen said, "and we had two brothers and two sisters who were older than either of us. I was the last child born to my mother, who, in bearing me, suffered a stroke that took away sight from her left eye, and sensation from much of the right side of her body so that she was unable to work in the fields from that time on. Such an affliction was not uncommon among our people, of course, for women suffered this and numerous other ailments during and after childbearing, whether the children survived or did not. In point of fact, before my first surviving brother was born, my mother had three sons who died within their first year of life.

"My father was, at my birth, doubly disappointed—first, because he had wanted another son, and, second, because his wife was no longer of utility to him and to our family. It is not surprising, then, that he took out his disappointments on me, beating me regularly, though not, in my early years, savagely. He beat me the way he did, it seems to me now, more out of obligation than anger—out of a sense of what his paternal duty was toward a child who had brought misfortune to his family. He seemed, most times, bored with the task, as he was with me, and he also withheld from me the affection that he bestowed, albeit irregularly, upon my older brothers and sisters. It was James, however, his youngest and last son, who became the favorite, much as Benjamin was to the patriarch Jacob.

"That was the year we picked up our worldly belongings and traveled west, taking odd jobs along the way—field work and whatever day labor was available—until we landed on the outskirts of Kinnard, Texas, where my mother's sister, Carrie, her husband, Charles, and their eleven children lived. They provided us with a one-room cabin behind their house, a cabin that had until our arrival been used for storage of farming tools and supplies. In addition to working some half-dozen acres of land, my aunt was employed as wet nurse to white families, and my uncle, in town, as helper to a blacksmith, while my older cousins worked my aunt and uncle's farm, took care of the house and younger children, tended to the animals that were theirs—one cow, one mule, two hogs, and chickens—and did seasonal work for local farmers and store-owners. My siblings and I were employed at various tasks my aunt and uncle obtained for us, and these tasks, along with our farm work, enabled us to earn our keep.

"Our quarters were close—James and I shared burlap-and-rag beds with our siblings—and our father, beholden to his brother-in-law, Charles, for work and sustenance, resented his dependency, of which my Uncle Charles reminded him daily. At the same time, my father's love of alcohol, which had been restrained in Louisiana, now prospered, as did his habit, when drunk, of beating me and my mother with increasing frequency and fury. He beat me, as I have said, for not being the son he had longed for, and also, as I grew older, for being the image of my mother—we did look alike, especially in the reddish tint of our skin, and in our high cheekbones—and he beat my mother, as before, for being a useless burden, and—more—for having brought him to a place where, ruled by the whims of his brother-in-law, he was subject to humiliation on a daily basis.

"I will spare you additional details of our family life, much of which Horace has learned, so that I may tell you of James, and of how he died, and of what his death inspired in me. Perhaps because he was our father's favorite, James possessed a sense of entitlement—and a will—at least equal to that of our father, and when he came of an age, this at fifteen years old, where his physical size was also equal to that of our father, he began standing up to him.

" 'If you choose ever again to lift a hand against my mother or sister, you will have to lift it against me first,' " he declared on a Sunday morning when we had returned from a local church gathering.

"Our father roared at James to get out of his way or he would kill him. My other brothers tried to intervene, but our father grabbed his whip and warned them that his wrath could fall upon them too. Still, when our father moved toward me and my mother— we were pleading with James to leave us be—James stood fast. Our father struck out at him with the whip, but drink had, mercifully, left him unbalanced, and the lash of the whip missed James entirely. When our father drew it back a second time, James simply stepped forward, removed the whip from our father's hand, and told him that it was the Lord's Day, and that we should honor it by doing what the Lord had done when, after six days, he had looked upon his work and seen that it was good: we should rest.

"Such a scene repeated itself intermittently for several months until one Sunday, our father, having put aside his drinking, greeted us upon our return from church as if he were himself a minister of

God—he could be a fiercely articulate man when sober—standing tall and quoting biblical scripture about the Lord declaring that a rebellious son should be brought before the elders of the village and, if declared rebellious, stoned to death.

"I stepped in front of James. My Uncle Charles then grabbed my father's arm, and snatched away the whip. We were family, he declared, and he would not permit any harm coming to us on the Lord's Day. For a brief moment, I was heartened, but then Charles seized James roughly, and told him that it was not a son's place to tell a father what he could and could not do to a wife or daughter. The children of a man's loins, along with the wife who had begat those children, he declared, were a man's property and, thus, obliged to do his will.

"Our father howled in triumph, and walked away, leaving us unharmed, but on the following Sunday, after church services, when James was gone off with his brothers to rest and smoke in the fields, our father found me with my mother, and began whipping us with a willow switch. I tried to protect my mother, who was helpless before his attack, and for so doing received numerous cuts across my arms, breasts, and back. When James returned and found us huddled together, our mother barely conscious, he tended to us, after which he went and found our father, who had neither whip nor switch in hand, and he beat our father until our father's face was unrecognizable.

"Later, when we were asleep—sometime after midnight—our father began banging upon the inside walls of our cabin with a rake and yelling '*Fire! Fire! Our house is on fire! Run for your lives!*'— and though his words were slurred by drink, they were, we quickly saw from clouds of smoke rising around us, true. And so we grabbed what possessions we could, fled from our home, and watched flames consume our dwelling. Neighbors soon arrived, and we did what we could—the women and children forming a bucket brigade, the men digging a trench between our house and the house in which Uncle Charles and his family lived—yet it was only when, the first light of dawn showing on the eastern horizon, and our cabin now become blackened timbers and ash, that I realized I had not seen James among us throughout the ordeal. Nor had I heard his voice.

"I made my way through the ruins to the far side of our home, where we kept our hog and chickens, all of whom, to my surprise, had been set free, and I found James there, sitting in a chair to which he had been tied with rope, his mouth a black oval of charred fabric. I fell to my knees, embraced my brother's scorched legs even while aware of the sweet fragrance of his burnt flesh, and before I could scream or weep or know *what* to do, my father's hands were upon me, lifting me up, muttering words about the vengeance of the Lord, and then, with hands wrapped in rags, tearing away the ropes that bound James to the chair, and pulling the blackened cloth from his mouth, after which he pushed what was left of James to the ground, shouting: '*James! James! I have found my son James! Oh help me! Help me! I have found my son James!*' And when others arrived, he continued to cry out, '*Oh James, my son, my son . . . Oh James, my son!*'"

"I didn't know, Joleen," Max said. "I am just so sorry—so terribly sorry . . ."

I was about to echo Max's words when I suddenly realized that what Joleen had been describing had never occurred. While she was telling her story, though, I believed it since it did not seem possible that anyone could simply have made it up.

"We kept a supply of lye powder on the east side of our cabin, the lye buried in a tight metal container, away from the animals, for lye powder when exposed to the air could quickly turn to liquid," Joleen continued. "We used the lye powder—the flakes—for the making of soap, for the cleaning, twice yearly, of our kitchen utensils, and, when we mixed it with water and mineral oil, for the care and straightening of our hair. We were warned early in life, and repeatedly, of how dangerous lye could be if allowed to penetrate skin or eyes, and whenever we retrieved it from the ground, we put on thick gloves and covered our faces.

"And so on a broiling summer day ten days after we had buried James, I pleaded dizziness and fatigue while working in the fields, and returned home—we were by then living in a room behind Aunt Carrie and Uncle Charles's house—knowing I would, except for our mother, be alone there. My mother tended to me with washcloths and a bittersweet drink made of tea leaves and ginger root, and then she lay down in a cool spot in our cabin—as cool a spot as one could find—and I talked her to sleep, telling her what I did not believe to be true: that James was resting with the angels in heaven and smiling down upon her.

"I dug out the lye and prepared a liquid solution, which I placed in a clay jar, for lye could eat through glass, and I hid the jar under branches beside a pecan tree not far from the table that was set outside the kitchen where, in the shade of large blackjack oaks, we ate most of our meals during the hot summer months.

"After Uncle Charles said grace, I retrieved the clay jar, and carried it to the table as if bearing food. My father actually smiled at me when I stood beside him—a rare event, and I do not deign to guess what it was in that moment that caused him to look at me in a kindly manner—and when he did, I opened the jar and, speaking words I had previously rehearsed—'*This will enable you to see—oh yes, to see the evil you have done to my brother James!*'—I flung the lye into his face.

"He clawed at his eyes, fell to the ground howling, and while my Aunt Carrie and the others crowded around him, I backed away from the table. Nobody moved to touch me, or to hold me, or strike me, or question why I had just done what I had done."

"*Jesus!*" Max exclaimed. "Jesus F. Christ, Joleen . . ."

"Jesus had nothing to do with it," Joleen said.

"Dear God, Joleen . . ." I began, and was about to ask how she could have committed such an act, but a sly smile at the corner of her mouth reminded me that she was inventing this tale in order, or so I reasoned, for Max to believe she had once had a brother who was no more, and who, alive or dead, was not me.

"And so I left home, and found work and shelter where I could, until I had the good fortune to meet Horace, whose love for me and faith in me enabled me to find a better road than the one I had been on," Joleen said. "The years that passed between my leaving home and meeting Horace are but a dream now, whatever the true events of those years may have been. What you should know about them, however, is that the one great and enduring regret that was born then, and that has stayed with me ever since, is that we did not, James and I, before his passing from this world, give and take pleasure from one another in the manner we have known."

Max backed away as if retreating from a fighter who had rocked him with punches to the gut and was moving in to finish the job. "You really *are* a nut job," he said. "Like I said before, you're bonkers—totally bonkers, and mean to boot."

"Those were not the words you spoke before," Joleen said.

"Yes or no, you're still a loon," Max said, and, turning away from Joleen, grabbed me by the back of the neck and pulled my face close to his. "So tell me this, Horace—this crazy woman—is she *really* your wife?"

The mad, bewildered look in Max's eyes was so wild I feared he might sink his teeth into my face. I seized the hand that held me and pried it away.

Max looked at his hand as if surprised to see it there. Then, shaking his head from side to side, he spoke to me in a low, slow voice: "Sorry," he said. "Sorry, Horace—I get carried away sometimes, right?—but what I mean is—did you *know* any of this stuff before you married her—what she wanted to do with James—with her own *brother*?"

"Not in the way I have learned today," I said. "But . . ." I paused, while Max's eyes implored me to tell him something—anything!— that would allow him to make sense of what he had heard. "I have always known of my wife's love of the Bible," I continued "—and have sometimes sensed that although the tales from the Bible are religious in nature—written by God, or to praise God—her love of Bible stories—of The Song of Solomon, which is her favorite—has had more to do with the pleasure human beings give and take from one another when they are in love."

"That's good news," Max said. "Not to make light of your brother's death, Joleen, but I can buy what you're saying about regret. I can buy that big-time."

He chucked me gently on the cheek, then took Joleen's hands in his.

"I'm real sorry for your loss, and for what you lived through," he said to her. "So what I'm gonna do, see, is when I fight the fight that's gonna make me heavyweight champion of the world, I'm gonna dedicate the fight, and my victory, to your brother James. That's what I'm gonna do."

Max was true to his word. While he trained for the championship fight against Carnera, who had won the title a year earlier by knocking out Jack Sharkey with an uppercut that, according to those at ringside, never touched Sharkey's jaw, he talked about James every day. "I'm gonna win the fight for James, and for your wife," he would say. "I'm gonna turn that simple-minded lug to ashes—and when I say ashes I don't mean the kind they haul away after a night with a lady friend."

Carnera, however, fifty pounds heavier and five inches taller than Max, was an early favorite, the bookmakers setting the odds against Max at more than two to one, and with reason. Following on his victory against Schmeling, Max was having too good a time to be bothered by working out regularly. Once the championship bout was scheduled—a first for him—Max went an entire year without fighting a single fight. And while Max was staying away from the ring, Carnera was busy defending his title, going the distance of fifteen rounds against two excellent boxers—Paolino Uzcudun, former European heavyweight champion, and Tommy Loughran, former world light-heavyweight champion—thereby demonstrating how seriously he took his conditioning, and the responsibility to be a *fighting* champion.

Six weeks before the title fight, we set up our training camp in Asbury Park, on the New Jersey shore, but beginning with our first day there Max was more interested in the women who walked the boardwalk than in his speed bag or sparring partners. Even when William Brown, a member of the New York State Boxing Commission, arrived to see if rumors he was hearing were true—that Max was turning our training camp into a circus—Max continued to be Max. When Brown threatened to cancel the fight, and declared Max "a bum," Max laughed. "I got some ancient wisdom for you, my friend, to help you with the little woman you got waiting for you at home," he said to Brown, when a group of reporters had gathered around. "And here it is: 'Confucious say that foolish man give wife grand piano, but wise man give wife upright organ.'"

A few minutes later, as if to prove how fit he was, Max, already in a dapper outfit—blue blazer, fawn-colored slacks, black-and-tan dancing shoes—proceeded to lift his brother Buddy, who weighed nearly two hundred and fifty pounds, above his head, spin him around, set him down, and do so without even breathing hard. The following afternoon, Max held court as he did most afternoons, and when a writer who had been covering Carnera reported that Carnera was in top-notch condition, Max said that was fine with him, because it meant he'd get more credit when he licked him. "Listen, if it wasn't meant for me to be heavyweight champion of the world, I wouldn't be here," he said. "No kidding." And then, quietly, what he had said to me in private, but had never said to others: "I don't *like* fighting, you know."

Astonished by Max's statement, the writers tried to get him to explain what he meant, but the only thing Max did was to repeat what he had said, without apology, and to add, as if he were talking about going out to buy a cup of coffee or a morning newspaper, that if the main idea was to go out there and knock the other guy down— well, he could do *that*.

"So if you bozos don't have any more questions," he said, "I'm gonna head out now and show my brother how to have a good time in this town."

At the weighing-in ceremony four days before the fight, Max, arriving late, and in his finest white linen outfit, sat down next to Carnera, who, stripped to the waist, was sitting on an examining table. Max winked at the reporters, plucked a hair from Carnera's chest and held it up for all to see. "*He loves me!*" he proclaimed. And before Carnera could respond, Max had plucked a second hair from Carnera's chest. "Aw," he said, "he loves me not . . ."

In truth, although I enjoyed Max's antics, like others, I was concerned, for not only was he seemingly disinterested in the fight itself, but the part of him that feared inflicting harm on others was showing itself forth with alarming frequency. Before sleep each night and upon waking each morning, he talked with me about Joleen and her brother James. How could it be, he would ask, that human beings could hurt one another in the ways they did. How could it be that a father could burn his own son to death, and how could a good woman like Joleen live with the knowledge she had made her own father—despicable and deserving of punishment though he was—blind? Then, sensing my unease about his readiness for the upcoming fight, he would reassure me, saying that there was nothing to worry about because he knew exactly what he was doing and why. When he entered the ring against Carnera, he was going to be thinking not of what he had done once upon a time to Campbell and Schaaf, but of what Joleen's father had done to James, and this would enable him to be every bit the monster Carnera was said to be.

Despite constant pleas from his trainer, Cantwell, and his manager, Hoffman, to attack his sparring partners, when he had one of us on the ropes (I continued, occasionally, to spar with him), or had stung one of us with a crushing blow that left us helpless, Max would simply back away. When a reporter accused him of lacking the requisite "viciousness" to be a true champion, Max replied with a simple statement, and without the least bravado: "Hey—I feel great. I'm no gymnasium fighter, see—so I don't want to hurt any of my sparring partners." He shrugged, and continued in a low, even voice: "But I'll go after Carnera all right. You can count on it. I'm going to be the champion, and don't say I didn't tell you."

Before dawn on the day of the bout, his head resting on my chest, Max said that although what he'd been saying—that he didn't like boxing, and that he didn't want to hurt others—was true, because of what he'd done to Campbell and Schaaf, who would ever believe him? So what he wanted to know—the only thing that truly mattered to him—was this: if he won the fight in memory of Joleen's brother, would *she* understand that he'd done what he'd done not out of some eye-for-an-eye thirst for revenge, but out of love and respect for *her*, and a desire to ease *her* pain?

On the evening of June 14, 1934, while more than seventy thousand raucous fans in the Madison Square Garden Bowl in Long Island City waited for the championship bout to begin, the same men said to have paid for Sharkey's magical fall to the canvas against Carnera entered our dressing room, informed Max that they represented Owney Madden's interests, patted bulges in their jacket pockets, and said that Madden was seeking assurances that by the end of the evening Carnera would still be heavyweight champion of the world. Max, on the massage table, face down, getting a rubdown, didn't even look up. "You take care of this, okay, Jerry?" he said, and Max's bodyguard, Jerry "Iron Neck" Cassell, opened his jacket to reveal the pistol he kept in his waistband. "Get out," he said, and Madden's men, seasoned thugs that they were, did. As soon as they were gone Max sat up and said something other fighters in similar situations had said before him—words first made famous by the great Barney Ross—"What are they gonna do—kill me?" he laughed. "Hey—everybody dies."

An hour later, to deafening cheers and thunderous foot stamping, Max climbed through the ropes and entered the ring, and he did so wearing a silk robe not with his own name on its back, but with the name "Steve Morgan," the character he had played in *The Prizefighter and the Lady,* embroidered there. And on his trunks, as in the fight against Schmeling, but on the left leg this time, was a glistening, coal-black Star of David.

Despite all those who had doubted his conditioning and his will, or perhaps to shame those who had questioned both, he proceeded to destroy Carnera, knocking him down three times in the first round and three times again in the second. Carnera stumbled around the ring like a drunken clown, trying in vain to protect himself, and grabbing onto the ropes constantly, thereby leaving his large body open to the lightning fury of Max's blows. Between rounds, Max joked with people at ringside, and waved to the crowd, and once, when he had leveled Carnera with a one-two combination—a solid smash to the gut, and a clean right hook to the jaw—and Carnera, falling, had pulled them both to the canvas, Max shouted out for all to hear, "Hey—last one up's a sissy!"

In the tenth round, Max hammered Carnera to the canvas three more times, and begged the referee, Art Donovan, to end the fight. "Hey Art," he said. "Please stop it. *Please*? Carnera's helpless." Despite Max's plea, Donovan let the fight continue. In the eleventh round, however, when Max had, without savagery but with crisp efficiency, floored Carnera yet two more times, Donovan, who would later claim it was Carnera who asked him to stop the fight, was left with no choice but to step between the fighters (Carnera, sobbing away afterwards, something no one had ever seen a champion do, denied he had made the request, and swore he would *never* have given up). Seconds later, the ring announcer took Max's right hand in his own, raised it high, and declared Maximilian Adelbert Baer the new and undisputed heavyweight champion of the world.

The crowd chanted its approval—"*Max! Max! Max!*" they cried out again and again—and Max skipped around the ring, blew kisses to everyone, and even performed a quick, graceful soft-shoe dance of the kind he'd done in *The Prizefighter and the Lady*. In our dressing room a few minutes later, he continued to have the time of his life, joking with reporters and, with mock seriousness, telling them he was truly glad he hadn't been up to commissioner Brown's conditioning standards or there might have been a *real* tragedy in the ring. And when reporters asked him who his current sweetheart was—Jean Harlow or June Knight, Bee Star or Shirley La Belle— Max declared that his only sweetheart was his mother.

"And what a sweetheart she is," he went on. "Wouldn't think of suing me for breach of promise. And boy, what an advantage that is since dames have already cost me more than a hundred thousand bucks!"

When asked if rumors were true that he'd taken up with Dorothy Dunbar again, he said that he thought their having been separated seven times was enough. "Besides," he laughed, "I'm too young to get married again."

Then Max put on a fawn-colored gabardine suit, a brown-and-white striped shirt, a brown-and-white striped necktie, a new pair of tan toe-cap oxford shoes, and, with Buddy, Jack Dempsey, Jerry Cassell, me, and the rest of our entourage, he went out on the town—to the Stork Club, Toots Shor's, the Cotton Club, and other favorite haunts, where, on that night, and all day the next day, and on the days and nights that followed, he rejoiced in the good wishes of others—Jews especially, who claimed him, with his blessing, as *their* champion—the first Jewish heavyweight champion ever—and where, for all those fortunate enough to know him, his boundless energy and spirit transformed New York City into a New Jerusalem of joy—a pleasure dome of luxurious indulgences unlike any I had known before, or have known since.

When, ten days later, the time came to pack up and head cross-country for Livermore, he surprised me with the news that we would, for a while, be parting ways. Mickey B. Friedman, who had been Max's stand-in during the making of *The Prize Fighter and the Lady*, would take his place on the west-bound train while Max slipped away, disguised as a bearded Bible salesman, and headed south for Washington, DC. There, his public words about marriage notwithstanding, he was going to pay court to a woman he'd met a few months earlier, Mary Ellen Sullivan, and see if she was who he believed she was: the girl of his dreams who was going to make the great dream of his life come true.

"But your dreams *have* come true," I said. "You're the heavyweight champion of the world, in addition to which you have already met, several times over, the girl of your dreams, and have even married one of them . . ."

"Ah, but none of them till now have made my heart do somersaults the way she does," he said. He kissed me softly on the cheek. "You know me well, Horace—you and your wife know me better than anyone—so I can level with you the way I can't level with anyone else, but the *real* dream is to be the champ, which I've done, but also to be the champ with a woman I love by my side—a woman who can help me bring some fabulous baby Baers into the world. And guess what? I think I found her!"

I congratulated him without voicing my skepticism, and I wished him well on his journey. I said that I had been favorably impressed with Miss Sullivan when we had met her at the Willard Hotel in Washington, where she was the manager of its coffee shop. She had a sweetly sassy way about her that had endeared her to us both, so that I could truthfully say to Max that, like him, I had become fond of her.

"And you know what it's gonna be like, me and her and baby-makes-three out at the ranch—what I figured out, dumb me?"

"Pray tell me," I said.

"Why, it's gonna be so wonderful, it's gonna be almost—" he paused "—*unbearable*! That's how wonderful it's gonna be! Completely and totally un-*baer*-able! Get it?"

Then he laughed, embraced me again, and while he did, my thoughts turned to Joleen, and to how news of Max's new lady-love—or of the possibility of marriage to this woman—might affect her. When he asked if I realized that what he was giving me was "a genuine and undisputed heavyweight championship Baer hug," though, I could not help but pull him close to me and wish him well.

Upon my return to the Baer ranch, I found Joleen to be as she had been before: quiet, sullen, distant. She performed her chores well and efficiently, and was respectfully affectionate with me in ways a wife was expected to be with a husband, but other than perfunctory exchanges—about the weather, about work accomplished and work still to be done—and muted expressions of congratulation on Max's triumph, along with token inquiries as to his whereabouts and plans, she showed little interest in anything beyond the essentials of daily living: eating, working, sleeping.

On the third day of my third week back home, however (Max was still, as far as anyone knew, in Washington, DC), I returned to our cabin from a sparring session with Buddy on what was, for California in summer, a refreshingly mild late afternoon in July, to be greeted by a strange aroma. Joleen was sitting on the floor at the foot of our bed, in the dark—I mistook her, at first, for a shadow—her face covered with what seemed to be gray powder, but which, I saw upon closer perusal, were ashes.

The crate in which she had kept her dolls was bare.

I knelt beside her and instead of asking what she had done, I phrased my question, and concern, as a statement: "You have burned your dolls," I said.

"You are a wise and observant brother," Joleen said.

"But why—and why now?"

"Why? In order that my ghosts truly *be* ghosts," she said. "Why now? Because you are home, and I am safe again. I know you will protect me."

"Protect you from *what*?"

For the first time since I had returned to Livermore, she smiled at me, and when she did I felt my heart surge with a love for her that I had for some time forsworn.

She took my hands in hers and kissed them. "The dark beast that has been pursuing us has made its home in my heart," she said. "Therefore—in this way—will I keep him from making his home in yours."

"Because you love me?" I said.

"Because I love you," she said.

She rose from the floor and, her arms around my neck, her body warm against mine, she recited a verse from The Song of Solomon: " 'We have a little sister, and she hath no breasts; what shall we do for our sister in the day when she shall be spoken for?' "

I answered, as did the brothers in The Song of Solomon: " 'If she be a wall, we will build upon her a palace of silver; and if she be a door, we will inclose her with boards of cedar.' "

"Yes," she said, and she kissed me lightly on the lips. "And now lie down with me, my brother—lie down with a woman in whose heart the dark beast, whose vile desires will not be denied, rejoices."

Max returned to the ranch the last week in August, ebullient as ever, and bearing news: first, that he had agreed to fight an exhibition bout against King Levinsky in Levinsky's home town, Chicago. "Levinsky's a real hundred per cent Yid, not like me," Max said, "so that every Jew west of the Mississippi, and then some, are gonna show up, and the Kingfish and I are gonna give them a show they'll remember for the rest of their lives."

His second, happier piece of news, about which he swore Joleen and me to secrecy, was that within a year, after he'd fought a few exhibitions to build up the gate for the first defense of his title, and to lay away some loot for the Baer babies who would soon be running around the ranch, he and Mary Ellen Sullivan would tie the knot.

Joleen offered him her hand. "Congratulations," she said. "I trust she will prove worthy of you."

"Hey," he said, moving to embrace Joleen, who stepped away and began dusting our books with an invisible cloth. "No need to pout or be glum, Joleen. This won't change nothing between us."

"Of course not," she said. "You will still be you, and I will still be me, and Horace will still be Horace."

"But Mary Ellen and me will be married!" Max exclaimed. "And then the four of us will start in making families, and our babes will play with each other and become friends too."

"And perhaps the beast in my heart that you took for your own, will destroy your dreams," Joleen said.

"What the hell are you talking about?" Max said. "We ain't got no beasts around here—hogs and cows, and some horses now— gorgeous horses for my father, from the purse Carnera brought in, which is *his* dream come true, see—so what's this you're talking about—?"

Joleen pushed Max against the wall, and kissed him passionately in a way that made me fear she would sink her teeth into him.

Then she took a step back, and began dusting the walls.

"Hey—thanks," Max said. "I mean, I guess that's the way you people congratulate friends when they bring good news."

"I think not," I said, and I took Max by an arm—seized it—and turned him toward me. "I think Joleen is suffering from what is known as a melancholic disposition, and I think she means what she says about the destruction of your dreams. I think we need to be discreet about how and when we reveal our wishes to her."

"My husband is a wise man," Joleen said, and she waved her phantom cloth at Max so that motes of dust seemed to emanate from it, gray specks that floated weightlessly in the waning light of day.

Max nodded. "I'm sorry for your troubles, Joleen," he said. "I love you like I love my own mother—like I love Horace—like I love—well—*all* the people I love. But I've known people in life who've had the black willies and believed they'd never be happy again, but I'm here to tell you that you're gonna be happy again, and you and me and Horace are gonna have good times like always."

"May your words find their way into God's cold, unforgiving heart," Joleen said.

"You got that right," Max said. "And I swear to you that though me and Mary Ellen are gonna get hitched and call it marriage because it will *be* marriage—we're doing it—*I'm* doing it—mostly so I can bring some baby Baers into this crazy world."

"How sweet," Joleen said. "Have you inquired of *them*, and gained *their* approval for your decision?"

Max took a deep breath before he spoke again. "And here's something I been thinking and hoped I wouldn't have to say out loud," he said. "But what I want is for things to be on the up and up with us the way they've always been, because compared to what I've known with you two, what I have and expect to have with Mary Ellen is more like a contract, okay? I mean, compared to what I have with you, like I said, it's just what I guess you'd call a long-term mutual arrangement."

"But legalized."

"*That's for the kids we're gonna have!*" Max shouted. "Don't you understand *anything* I've been saying?!"

"I understand everything you've been saying," Joleen said.

"Let me put it this way then," he said, and I saw that, fists clenched, he was trembling. "Mary Ellen is a good woman, and I know you and Horace are gonna like her—love her, I hope—but you'll always—always always—be first in my heart."

"What heart?" Joleen said, and saying this, she walked out of our cabin, and toward the fields where his father's new horses were grazing.

Three days before the new year of 1935, Max entered the ring against King Levinsky at Chicago Stadium for what was to be the first of five exhibition fights. Although Max could lose his championship title in such an exhibition bout if (and only if) an opponent were to knock him out, the object of such exhibitions in those days was to provide a first-rate show for boxing fans while bringing in good money for promoters and the champion. And traveling around the country and having good times between championship bouts was the ideal life for Max. Levinsky, however, who had defeated fighters such as Jack Sharkey and Tommy Loughran, and who was managed by his sister, Lena "Leaping Lena" Levy, had ideas Max had not anticipated.

When the bell rang for round one, and the fighters met in the middle of the ring, Max laughed and, as if preparing to annihilate Levinsky with a single punch, performed an elaborate windmill windup with his right arm, at which point Levinsky stepped forward and slammed the hardest right hook he could to Max's jaw.

Max, playing along, wobbled around the ring as if he'd been hurt badly, then thrust his chin forward to give Levinsky an easy target, whereupon Levinsky again punched Max in the jaw. "*Hey!*" Max screamed at him. "*We're supposed to be having fun!*" So they danced around together for the first round, Max keeping Levinsky away with nifty jabs and nimble footwork, but when, at the start of round two, Levinsky strode to the center of the ring, and gestured mockingly for Max to come and get him, Max had had enough. "That's it," he said to Cantwell, and he charged at Levinsky, and pounded him—left right, right left, left right—then finished him off with a crushing right that sent Levinsky to the canvas, where he was counted out, and from which he had to be carried to his corner.

"He thought he could sneak in and make himself king," Max said to reporters afterwards, "but I turned that blowhard into a dead fish." And when the reporters peppered him with questions about his romances, and asked if it was true that he was engaged to one of his new sweethearts, not Mary Ellen Sullivan, but Mary Kirk Brown, a New York café society lady, he laughed. "I know many girls," he said, "many lovely girls. But I think I shall still order *à la carte* for a while."

And so he did. He courted many ladies, and he also continued to court Mary Ellen Sullivan, traveling to Washington, DC, when we were nearby, and sometimes when we were not, and twice hiring private planes to get him there so that the two of them could work at persuading her family, who were devout Catholics, to accept Max as a son-in-law.

In mid-February, Max fought and won a second exhibition bout, in San Francisco's Dreamland arena, this time against Stanley Poreda, a heavyweight contender who'd beaten both Carnera and Schaaf, all proceeds from the fight, Max's purse included, going to a trust fund Max had set up for Frankie Campbell's widow and son. And Max's generosity extended beyond the Campbell family, and his own family: he loved giving away money the way he loved having a good time. He would get two hundred and fifty dollars in a cash allowance from Hoffman (who tried in vain to control Max's extravagances), and give it away within an hour to a bum on skid row, or a guy in line at a soup kitchen. Several times I watched him give down-and-outers the very shirts and jackets off his back. "He has a heart bigger than his body," his sister Maudie once said to me, and it was true. And he was as generous to others—to his parents especially, for whom he bought a new home near Oakland, in the East Bay town of Piedmont—as he was to his brothers and sister, to Joleen and me, to Mary Ellen, and, as ever, to himself. He bought clothes, cars, and gifts for everyone—he was a great free spirit, and as this first (and only) championship year drew toward its end, what I began to understand was that he was freer than ever because, having had one of his dreams come true—becoming heavyweight champion of the world—he could let go of parts of his life that had led to the championship—the training, the deal making, the fights themselves—and, quite simply, do what he wanted.

After he had moved his parents to Piedmont, Max kept Twin Oaks mainly, he told others, so that Buddy, Augie, and Maudie could continue to enjoy it, but his real reason was so that Joleen would have a place in which to live that felt familiar, and in which she felt safe, for in that sublimely carefree and happy year—a year in which he fought only exhibition matches—the only dark cloud that shadowed his life, as it did mine, came from the fear that the beast Joleen claimed had made its home in her heart might persuade her to leave this world and join her brother James.

Max and I returned to Livermore on four other occasions that year, and each time we did, the first thing Max did was to visit Joleen, who remained as she had been—sad, brooding, silent. Still, Max was able to coax her into taking long walks with us on the property, and what surprised me was that he did not force conversation upon her, or ever—a sign of a sensibility few could have guessed at—ask her how she was feeling, or why she was sad, or what he could do to help. He simply attended to her and, now and then, told her of some incident that had occurred during our travels—usually a comic incident in which he had played the fool.

When the three of us picnicked in meadows where the horses and cows grazed, he would talk about places we had seen and good times we had had, and about how, win or lose in defense of his title (for he had reluctantly agreed, in April, to fight, again in Long Island City's Madison Square Garden Bowl, against a journeyman heavyweight named James J. Braddock, who had lost twenty-one of his eighty-three fights), he was looking to get out of the fight game so he could make more movies, play the nightclubs, and, most important of all, start a family he intended to raise right here on the ranch.

"You don't have a mean bone in your body, do you, Max?" I recall Joleen saying to him one afternoon in May when we were enjoying a midday picnic under a stand of pecan trees in the ranch's furthest meadow.

"That's what my mom always said," Max said.

"Yet in the boxing ring you compensate for this deficiency of character admirably," Joleen said.

Max laughed. "I like the way you put it," he said. "But yeah—if it's for all the marbles, then I gotta make sure I get the other guy before he gets me. Only . . ."

"Only what, Max?"

"Only I still think about that poor kid Campbell and what I did to him," Max said. "It's not like me, you know."

"But it *is*," Joleen said. "We are what we do, after all, though your mother has often said that, grateful as she is for the good life you have brought to the family, she can never get used to seeing you as the man you have become since you were, she claims, a somewhat shy, even cowardly boy who never liked fighting."

"That's true enough," Max said. "But it'll be over soon. I won't ever throw no fight—I'm not a quitter, you can bet your life on that—but if—and it's not the only reason—but if it can help you back to the Joleen you used to be, then that's gonna help me do what I was gonna do soon anyway, which is to walk away from it all."

"What you do or don't do will not alter who I am or how I choose to lead my life," Joleen said, starting to walk away. "I will always love you, Max Baer—whether you fight or don't fight, or whether you win or you lose."

Max prepared for his fight against Braddock even more lackadaisically than he had for the fight against Carnera. Still, he entered the ring as a ten-to-one favorite. Braddock, who had a reputation for being a plodder—slow-footed and slow-witted—was by now considered what we called "a tomato can," meaning a washed-up fighter against whom an up-and-coming fighter might build a reputation, or a champion might fight in order to stay in shape and to keep the money rolling in.

Less than a year before, to support his wife and three children, Braddock had been working on the docks for five dollars a day and, when there was no work, had suffered the humiliation of going on relief. Following a leave-taking from boxing of nine months, he had, upon only two days notice, been given a chance to be a setup for a boxer on the rise named "Corn" Griffin, against whom he scored a surprise technical knockout in the third round, and after which, between stints as a dock worker, he had defeated two other good fighters, John Henry Lewis and Art Laskey, in a series of elimination bouts that had earned him his shot at Max.

On the night of the fight, Braddock came out fighting, and Max came out clowning. Max's old habit—letting his hands drop to his sides either to hitch up his trunks, or to tempt the other fighter to attack—became a weakness Braddock exploited relentlessly. And Max was, simply, tired, his fatigue due in large part to having locked everyone out of his dressing room before the fight in order to have his pleasure with one of his new lady friends, an event that made reporters gleeful, and Hoffman insane with rage. And in the ring, he seemed surprised that no matter what he did—moving in circles around Braddock, flicking away jabs with a stiff, outstretched left arm, or faking a jab and then trying to move in with a series of uppercuts—Braddock just kept coming, his head burrowed into Max's shoulder while he pushed Max around the ring, backing off now and then in order to land solid lefts and rights, and then coming at Max again.

Between the fifth and sixth rounds, Max whispered to me that he didn't know how he could knock Braddock out (which he saw as his only hope, since Braddock was far ahead on points and, as Max continued to tire, would doubtless increase his lead), because he was pretty sure he had broken his right hand. But whether he had broken the right hand and/or the left (after the fight, it turned out that he had, in fact, broken the right hand and badly damaged the left, information Max never revealed to the press), and whether he did or did not care about winning (Jack Dempsey was livid afterwards, writing in the *New York Times* about Max's "miserable defense of his title," and about how his "dilly-dallying and clowning had finally caught up with him"), he did summon up what stamina he had left, and fought his heart out in the final rounds of the fifteen-round bout, rounds in which neither he nor Braddock had the legs or power left to put the other fighter away.

Thus did James J. Braddock become the new heavyweight champion of the world—a hero to boxing fans, as well as to all who, in those Depression years, knew what it was like to be down and out, and to have to take charity in order to provide for their families. Max was gracious in defeat, praising Braddock, saying he knew he deserved to lose, and adding that he now planned to retire from boxing and raise white-face cattle on his ranch in Livermore.

Sixteen days after the fight, on June 29, 1935, Max and Mary Ellen Sullivan were married in the Washington, DC, home of Justice F. Dickinson Letts, who presided over a private ceremony I attended, and soon after, as Max had promised, he and Mary Ellen moved west to the Baer ranch.

His promise to retire from boxing, however, was short-lived. Although he continued to fight against the very best fighters in the world—Joe Louis, Lou Nova, Buck Rogers, and "Two-Ton" Tony Galento, among others—and to defeat all of them, with the exception of Joe Louis, who, in the presence of 95,000 people in the Yankee Stadium, destroyed Max in four rounds in the most punishing defeat of Max's career—he devoted himself increasingly to his life with Mary Ellen, and to his career on stage and screen. He developed a vaudeville routine with his friend, the former light-heavyweight champion Max "Slapsie Maxie" Rosenbloom, which they performed in many venues, including nightclubs Rosenbloom owned; he acted in movies—nearly two dozen of them in the ensuing years, including Humphrey Bogart's final movie, *The Harder They Fall*, whose main character, "the champ," was based on Max, and in the first-ever live ninety-minute television drama, *Requiem for a Heavyweight*; and he also earned numerous pay days as a disc jockey, a wrestler, and (as Jack Dempsey had done) a celebrity referee for both boxing and wrestling matches.

Then, on December 4, 1937, within a year and a half of their marriage, he and Mary Ellen became the proud parents of a son: Max Baer Jr. And Max Baer Jr.'s arrival in the world, which preceded Horace Jr.'s by a half year, changed our lives yet again, and forever, for until Max Baer Jr.'s birth, Joleen had continued to live in the unlit caves of her melancholic disposition. The only thing that seemed to brighten her days during these years had been books, and the acquisition of books. Our cabin overflowed with them—in bookcases I built and secured against walls, on wide-board planks under windows, and in boxes stored in our closet, above our kitchen cabinets, and under our bed—and the few times I saw light in her eyes, or heard lightness in her voice, were the times she would, with uncharacteristic timidity, ask if I had the time to listen to a passage she had come across in one of her books and thought I might find of interest. I would do so willingly, of course, and would from time to time suggest that perhaps she could renew her plan to be a teacher and thereby transmit her love of literature to others. No matter how tentatively or diplomatically I made such a proposal, however, she would respond each time by saying, "Oh no—that is not meant to be," after which she would return to her reading, her chores, and her brooding. From the instant Mary Ellen handed the newborn Max Baer Jr. to her, and Joleen held him in her arms, however, she was born again into the woman she had been before the beast of darkness had made her prisoner to his foul authority.

What seems curious, in retrospect, is that even as Max seemed, following upon his marriage to Mary Ellen, a changed man, frequently (and publicly) renouncing his life as a fighter in favor of his life as a husband and father-to-be, yet did he continue to fight, and to fight with *greater* frequency than ever. In the eighteen months between his defeat by Braddock and the birth of his son Max Jr., Max fought twenty-two fights, losing only twice (once to Louis, and once to British heavyweight champion Tommy Farr), scoring knockouts eleven times, and technical knockouts four times.

Since Max was not in need of money—he earned considerable sums from movies and vaudeville, from refereeing and public relations stunts (while Ancil Hoffman, investing wisely for him, doled out allowances so that Max's extravagances would not do him in)—I must conclude that, no matter his words about not liking to fight and not wanting to hurt others, yet did he truly love the sport known as the "sweet science."

And he loved the life that came with the sport: he loved the money; he loved the crowds; he loved the reporters; and he loved the nightlife and the ladies. To the surprise of many, as I have noted, he rarely consumed significant quantities of alcohol (our first meeting with him being an exception) because, he explained, he did not like to dull his senses, and—more important—his ability to remember, the morning after, just how good a time he had had the night before.

I also believe that he loved the fighting itself far more than he admitted or knew. I believe he loved being lost in an elemental passion for hitting and being hit—in the licensed savagery permitted when, before cheering and bloodthirsty fans, he was free to inflict violence upon another man without the least need to temper the violence with mercy—and he also loved the gratification that came with practicing a craft at which he was a master, and which, like the act of love, and the ecstasy of being in love, fed his desire to take as much pleasure from life as possible, so that the extended moments in which he could give free rein to his power and his desires, whether in the ring or in his romances, served to enhance and heighten his love of life itself.

The only fighter I have ever known who rivaled him in the sheer joy he took when in the ring—in the way he taunted and danced around his opponents (sometimes performing soft-shoe tap routines); in the way he "played possum"—pretending to be hurt, then surprising an opponent with a flurry of rapid-fire blows; in the way he let his guard down so as to invite the other fighter to attack; in the way he laughed when an opponent had landed a good blow against him; in the way he delighted in bantering with reporters before, after, and during bouts; and, most of all, in the joy he took from being able to give boxing fans a great, good time—was a fighter I had the privilege of seeing in action but once (four years after Max's passing), and whom Max, alas, never did see: a man whose physiognomy and coloring were not unlike my own, descended as we both may have been, to judge by appearances, from the legendary Falconhurst slaves—the great and distinguished champion Muhammad Ali.

3

Scenes from Childhood

*Let us get up early to the vineyards; let us
see if the vine flourish, whether the tender
grape appear, and the pomegranates bud
forth: there will I give thee my loves. (7:12)*

Horace Littlejohn Jr. was born at
eight minutes before six on the morning of May 30, 1938. I count
this the happiest moment of my life, for I sensed on that morning
that our son's birth would redeem for Joleen, even more than Max
Jr.'s birth had, those hours and days of her life that had been lost to
the dusky vapors of her depressive humors. Max and his wife, Mary
Ellen, along with Buddy Baer and Max and Buddy's mother, Dora,
were there with us, as was a local midwife, Miss JoAnna Butler,
whom Max had fetched shortly before midnight the evening before,
when, upon visiting us after he put Max Jr. to sleep, as was his habit
most evenings, he saw that Joleen had gone into labor, and that she
was, though valiantly denying it, in considerable pain.

Horace Jr. weighed six pounds two ounces at birth—nearly three pounds less than Max Baer Jr. had weighed at his birth—and he was, miracle of miracles, born with fingers and toes noticeably longer than seemed natural for a child of his size. His skin was a ruddy, somewhat splotched mocha brown, and he arrived with a full and impressive head of black curls, the curls made slick by the liquids that had accompanied him on his journey from the womb. Although Joleen, exhausted from her labors, showed nothing but a childlike contentment in holding her son close to her and having him, within minutes of his birth, suckle at her breasts, I expect she may have been as relieved as I was that Horace had not come into our world with the fair skin or facial features that would have suggested to attentive observers the true nature of his parentage.

And just as Abraham regarded Ishmael, son of his concubine Hagar, as his true son, so did Max Baer regard Horace Jr. as his son (though without acknowledging this to others). But whereas Abraham's wife, Sarah, childless until Ishmael was a young man, was jealous in the extreme of Hagar and Ishmael, and had Abraham banish them into the wilderness of Beersheba, an act intended by Sarah to cause their deaths (which deaths would, without God's merciful intervention, have surely occurred), neither Max nor Mary Ellen showed anything but love and kindness toward Horace.

And Max Baer Jr. loved our son Horace Jr., and our son Horace Jr. loved Max Baer Jr., and they grew up together on the Baer ranch and, later on, in the home Max and Mary Ellen made for themselves in Sacramento, where Joleen and I also came to reside in order that we might continue to serve in their employ. Not knowing they were true brothers, and without those envies and resentments that in families too often transform natural affections into less generous feelings, Max Baer Jr. and Horace Littlejohn Jr. became great, good friends to each other even as brothers sometimes are.

The years that followed, during which the boys grew from childhood to young manhood, and, when each was eighteen years old, left home—Max Jr. for Santa Clara University, and Horace Jr. for the University of California at Berkeley—were, in the large, good and fruitful years, and I feel confident in stating that we all would have agreed, without the need to express the thought in words, that these were years informed by that rarest of entities: family happiness. And this was due, above all, to *who they were*—to the fact that Max Baer Jr. and Horace Littlejohn Jr. were living incarnations of a truth to which many are blind: that who we are in our time on earth is not determined merely by the biological vector produced by the coupling of a man and woman, but by something else—by that essence within each of us that, independent of our parenting and/or our upbringing, is an irreducible and eternal self that is *I-and-no-other*.

Both boys were, in my estimation, possessed of intelligence beyond that of their parents, and both boys, early on, though as gifted as their coevals in matters athletic and academic, distinguished themselves at different activities. Max Jr., for example, considerably taller, more sturdy, and more outgoing than Horace, was highly proficient at football and baseball, and later on as an actor in theatrical productions, whereas Horace, possessed of remarkably quick hands and feet, and a nimble facility with words, excelled at basketball and track, and was the leading orator on his high school debate team. It was in their finely tuned sensibilities, however, that they were most alike. They were, each of them, fair-minded concerning others, including those against whom they competed, infinitely curious about the world, and—always, always—innately kind, taking to heart a saying from Philo of Alexandria (known also as Philo the Jew), taught to them by Joleen, which Horace Jr. translated as follows (and which he has on occasion recited for me in the original Greek): "Be kind, for everyone you meet is fighting a great battle."

Both boys learned to read before they entered school, and grew up loving to talk *about* what they read. And they both took delight in telling stories, whether the stories were recountings of tales read, accounts of actual adventures, or invented. And in their storytelling they were ever observant of, and attentive to, those around them— to Max, Joleen, and Mary Ellen; to aunts, uncles, cousins, and grandparents; to schoolmates; to visitors and guests from the worlds of boxing and entertainment—just as they were to the wonders of the natural world—to the animals, gardens, fields, lakes, streams, and forests that, due to Max's ongoing financial success, surrounded them throughout their growing up and their coming of age.

In setting down my memories, it has been my primary purpose to tell the story of Max Baer's life, and, in particular, of the love my sister Joleen and I had for him, and knew with him. Although tempted to indulge a desire to reminisce about events from the lives of Horace Jr. and Max Jr., especially their early years, I will leave the telling of such tales to them, knowing that my son, Horace Jr., for one, is more gifted than I in the making of stories, and in making sense *of* stories. I will, however, tell of an event in Horace Jr.'s child-hood that proved significant to his lifelong passion for the study of Scripture.

During the years we lived in Livermore, Mary Ellen took Max Jr. with her every Sunday morning to nearby St. Peter's Holy Ro-man Catholic Church, where he had been baptized, and, when we lived in Sacramento, to All Souls Church of the Sacred Heart, where, at seven years of age, he received first Holy Communion, accepting Jesus Christ in the Sacrament of the Holy Eucharist. And during these years, Joleen and I took Horace Jr. with us several times a month to the Church of Our Holy Saviour, a house of worship at-tended by people of color.

The last time Joleen, Horace Jr., and I attended church as a family, however—or rather, the first of many Sundays upon which we would *no longer* attend church as a family—occurred two Sundays before Christmas of 1942 (and four and a half months after Max and Mary Ellen's second child, James Manny Baer, was born).

Horace Jr. and I were already dressed in our Sunday best when Joleen announced that she had made a decision not to go to church on this morning, or ever again. Horace Jr. protested at once, but Joleen commanded him to hold his tongue, and to wait in the cabin while she talked with me—we were spending the weekend at the ranch in Livermore—and, taking me by the hand, she led me outside.

"Where the beast of darkness once made his home," she announced in words she had clearly prepared earlier, "the true spirit of the Lord now lives."

"And so?" I asked.

"And so I no longer feel a need for others, whether priests, ministers, or ministering angels, to intercede for me with our Lord," she replied. "I have, on this day, ceased forever to be a churchgoing woman."

"That may be," I said, "and I know that when you have resolved to do something, there is little chance of my persuading you to change your mind. But what about Horace? You saw how upset he was by your decision. He *loves* going to church, and looks forward to it all week long. He loves the singing—he loves being with other children—and—"

"This afternoon I will tell him the story of the destruction of the Temple," Joleen said, her voice an uninflected monotone, "and I will explain to him how the Hebrew people survived and sometimes flourished, as they do to this day, despite suffering and persecution, once they no longer *had* a holy temple, and once their caste of priests no longer had power over them."

I felt lost—or, more exactly, that Joleen would soon be lost to *me* unless I could find a way to draw her back home, although I wondered if anything I said or did would make a difference, for I sensed that her precious beast of darkness, disguised this time as the spirit of the Lord, was once again luring her into a dusky isolation that could destroy all the good that, since the births of Max Baer Jr. and Horace Jr., had been ours.

I spoke the words that came to me. "I know how much pleasure and comfort your books give you—your reading of the Bible and of books *about* the Bible—and that these are matters that have intrigued you as, from time to time, they have intrigued me," I said. "But I wonder what *use* such knowledge can be for Horace—what sense *any* child can make of such notions."

"Ah, but today I will tell him the story celebrated at this season in temples and homes throughout the world—the story of the victorious rebellion of the Maccabees against the Romans," Joleen said. "I will tell him of the restoration of the Temple—of the miracle of the lights—and I will teach him to trust in Our Lord by trusting to his own good heart."

"Horace may be brilliant, but he is still a *child*, Joleen," I said, my voice rising with my fear that Joleen had once again set out on a journey to places where her better angels dared not go. "Like Max Jr., he is still a boy like other boys, and if . . ."

"But he is not *like* other boys, Horace—can't *you* see that?" she said. "He has a mind—and a vision—beyond the ordinary. Have you not noticed how he does not accept things merely because others do, or because others *claim* they are true? Have you not noticed, when we talk about Joseph and Mary, Jesus and Paul, or Abraham and Isaac, that no matter how enchanted he may be by the stories themselves, he always ends our talks by asking the same question?"

"Which is—?"

"How do we know this really happened?"

"But that's a question *any* child would ask—a question you and I asked when we were his age," I said. "And the answer we were given is the same all children are given: we know it happened—we *believe* it happened—because the Bible says it did, and because the Bible was written by the hand of God, and . . ."

"Oh Horace—was it *really?*" Joleen said. "And what is served by giving *any* child words that derive from ignorance and encourage ignorance? Tell me this, my brother: do you truly believe these stories *literally* took place in the way the Bible says they did, and were written down by that Being or Beings we have been worshipping?"

"Literally?" I said. "Perhaps not. But there is an essential truth in them that . . ." I stopped, then continued in a faltering manner: "If we believe . . . yes . . . and if we have faith, then the Bible can be our guide and our consolation, but . . ."

"Perhaps," Joleen said. "But even men of God—men of great learning and discernment—have expressed doubts, and have taught us to hearken to the stories and parables as if they were *all* of them parables—metaphors for living from which we might take meaningful lessons for our lives."

"True," I said. "Yet have you not said that you believe God's *greatest* gift to us has *been* metaphor? And if that is true, and if . . ."

Placing a finger upon my lips, Joleen gazed at me as if, once again, as in the years before we knew Max Baer, I was her pupil, and in that moment a wave of sadness washed through me, for I sensed that her decision not to attend church was irrevocably coupled to our love for one another. What I understood in this moment was something I had until now denied: the fact of her shame, and with it her belief in the eternal damnation that awaited her—a destiny that was a direct consequence of deeds she and I had committed once upon a time, and had persisted in committing.

Softly, I repeated words I had spoken a moment before: "If we believe and have faith, then the Bible can be our guide and our consolation. That is what I believe."

"Then do I now have *two* children?" she laughed. "Or perhaps three, if we count the biggest child of all—our friend and the father of our son's dearest friend, Maximilian Adelbert Baer. What do you think, my husband? Pray tell me, and please do so without your usual equivocations."

"As you wish," I said. "What I think is that you have, as *that* child said, lost your good sense. What I think—"

"Ah, but let us now put aside what *you* think, and pay attention to what our son thinks. It may be true, as our friend so delicately put it, that I am, now and again, bonkers—a true nut job, yes?—and that my mind does sometimes wander in realms to which, out of a spirit of loving-kindness, I do not invite my beloved companions to join me."

"Your munificence is exceeded only by your magnanimity," I said.

"And your ill-tempered humor is exceeded only by your bitterness, though your bitterness is surely justified," Joleen said. "You have, through the years, held your tongue admirably, and have given me the gift of an unconditional love that sometimes exists, when it exists at all, between a mother and child. And you have done this, let us recall, despite the fact that it was I who seduced *you*. I am grateful to you for your love and loyalty, but what is before us today is not our past, but a decision that will affect our son."

"*Our* son?" I said.

"Nor have I come to my decision out of pique or the spirit in me that is often contrary for the sake of being contrary," Joleen continued. "Our son has begun trying to make sense of the stories and commandments he has grown up with, and I find myself no longer capable of defending its irrationalities to him."

"But you *love* the Bible, and always have," " I exclaimed. "And it is you who have transmitted this love to our son!"

"*Our* son, yes," she said, and she did so without any trace of bitterness or irony. "I love the Bible, Horace, but not nearly so much as *he* does, you see, and isn't that a true gift?"

"A gift?"

"In the way we want to know why the sun rises or sets, or the world came to be, just so does our son want to know how these stories came to be and if the people in them really lived once upon a time the way you and I do. That is the *gift*, Horace, don't you understand?"

"No," I said. And again: "No."

Joleen seemed unperturbed by my reply. "I love you, Horace, and so, in my heart you can do no wrong." She closed her eyes and recited a line from The Song of Solomon we had often recited to one another: " 'I am my beloved's, and my beloved is mine.' "

I nodded assent, but chose not to recite back to her the sobering line that followed upon the one she had recited: "Thou art beautiful, O my love, as Tirzah, comely as Jerusalem, terrible as an army with banners."

"Just so it has always been," she said. "From the moment I watched our mother bear you into this world, and soon after—sunlight bathing your face with holy light—when she smiled up at me, and offered you to me so that, as she often reminded me, child that I was myself, I could hold your soft life in my arms while she told me that I now I had a brother I could care for and love for the rest of my days."

Joleen pressed her lips to my forehead, and when she did I felt a stirring in my thighs and I was surprised, looking down, to see Horace Jr. there, his face pillowed against my leg.

"Am I your gift?" he asked, smiling up at me. "*Am* I?"

"Yes, my son, you are my gift," I said, lifting him up and holding him in my arms, "and your mother and I have decided not to go to church this morning so that we might have more time with one another."

"Is that so, Mother?" he asked.

"It is," Joleen said. "But this afternoon we *will* read from the Bible to one another, and you may invite Max Jr. to join us. Would you like that?"

I have set down the story of this day in my son Horace Jr.'s childhood, so that, reading it when I am no longer here, he can learn of matters that, notwithstanding his prodigious memory, he may not fully recall—and so that he may, thereby, better understand his own story, and something of the origins of his career as a Biblical scholar, which career has brought great honor to me and to Joleen as well as to Max, whose early passing from this world did not allow him to rejoice in the full flowering of Horace Jr.'s gifts.

What Max did rejoice in, however, was the fact of Horace Jr.'s existence, and of having *two* sons with whom he could set free his boundless exuberance. He would race across fields and meadows, one boy tucked under each arm, both of them shrieking with joy; he would roll around with the boys on the ground while screaming for others to come to his aid; he would have raucous tickling competitions with them, and declare each of them undisputed world champion; he would box with them, sing with them, dance with them, swim with them, and then, when one thought no child—or father—could sustain such rambunctious play a moment longer without collapsing in exhaustion, he would take one or the other of them into his arms, and lavish affection upon that child with gentle kisses and whisperings.

He would come to our cabin, or to our quarters in his home in Sacramento, lie in bed with Horace, and tell him stories about giant sea creatures and noble ship captains, about imaginary kings and kingdoms, and about brave boys who defended—with swords or bare knuckles—those who could not defend themselves. He would kiss both boys frequently in ways few men did—mouth on mouth— and he would take them on excursions into redwood forests and fishing villages north of San Francisco, or into San Francisco, where they would ride the trolleys, visit the zoo, sail out on fishing vessels, attend baseball games, and go to restaurants, theaters, and boxing gyms where men who adored and doted on Max would adore and dote on Horace Jr. and Max Jr.

When Max was on the road performing in theaters and night-clubs, or in Hollywood working on a movie, or far from home for a boxing match, a wrestling exhibition, or a publicity stunt, the boys would ask every day, and sometimes several times a day, about when he would be returning home.

Unlike Mary Ellen and Joleen, however, they were rarely forlorn while Max was away, and I do not recall either of them clinging to *what-was-not*, or to what they *could-not-have*; rather, they rejoiced in whatever was there for them to enjoy, whether separately, or with one another.

During these years, I here note, I enjoyed a moderately success-ful boxing career of my own, although it was neither my ambition nor my natural gifts, such as they were, that brought about this ad-venture whose brief life was directly tied to Max's own final hours as a professional prizefighter.

When we were on the road for one of Max's boxing matches, or when he was fighting an exhibition bout, or working as a celebrity referee, he would regularly urge me to put on my boxing gloves and do battle against others so that I could get onto the same card with him, and we could thereby take in a few extra dollars and celebrate our victories together afterwards. I had long ago forsworn any desire to fight professionally, but when everyone else, at home and away from home—Max's wife, his children, his handlers, his lady friends, his publicity agents, his coterie of journalists from the worlds of boxing, movies, and entertainment—were tearing off as many pieces of him as they could, my desire to draw him closer rose feverishly.

Then, late one sweltering August afternoon, after sparring together while he was in training for a bout in Jersey City against Pat Comiskey, he lavished praise on me again for my boxing prowess and stamina (he had called it a day when I was barely fatigued), and said he had been mulling over his idea again: that if I would let him book some fights for me, he would make *me* into a champion too.

"And how am I gonna do that?" he asked. "Why, by becoming your trainer, and—*my* reward, right?—getting to work those gorgeous buns of yours off on a regular basis."

He roared with laughter at his turn of phrase, but despite his vulgarity, which was of a familiar kind, and which irritated and offended me as, in its public variants, it often did others (he could not *not* persist in making jokes, often crude, of anything and everything), this time, weary of resisting his recurring propositions, I accepted his offer.

In the ring, I went by the name of "Frank 'Long-fingered' Joleen Jr.," in order, Max said when he bestowed the name upon me, to do honor to Frankie Campbell *and* to my wife and son. I fought four- and six-round preliminary bouts at first and, from my years of sparring with Max and Buddy, who were three weight classes above me (I fought as a welterweight, weighing in generally at between 155 and 158 pounds), I had little trouble disposing of fighters in my class. I won my first sixteen fights (including one against a former champion, the aging Jackie Fields), all by technical knockout or decision. I lacked Max's power, but remained, as ever, possessed of great quickness, good defensive instincts, and the ability to take advantage of my superior reach to score nearly two blows for every one received. By mid-January 1941, according to *Ring Magazine*, I was the twenty-third ranked fighter in my weight class, and discreet noises were made to Max, and to Ancil Hoffman, who had become my manager, about the possibility, within a year or two, of a title fight.

Less than three months later, however—on April 4, 1941—fighting in an eight-round bout in New York City's Madison Square Garden against an up-and-coming boxer named Pete Briscoe, an Irishman as strong as Braddock but with a quickness and killer instinct Braddock lacked, I was knocked down twice in the seventh round, at which point, though I was back on my feet doing nimble skip-steps by the count of four, the referee stepped in, stopped the fight, and declared Briscoe the winner by a technical knockout. I was far ahead on points with both judges, and Max and Hoffman immediately rushed into the ring, and began angrily accusing the referee of being on the take. No matter their protestations, and the crowd's lusty boos, the fight was over and lost, and with it, my unblemished record.

Max was the headliner that night, in a return bout against Lou Nova, a young contender who had beaten Max two years before (his only defeat since his loss on points, in 1937, to Tommy Farr in London), having scored a technical knockout against him in the eleventh round of a scheduled twelve-round bout. Max had balked at the decision, and had pleaded with the referee to let him continue, and in this second fight against Nova, he was as game as ever, but also as out of shape as ever, frequently joking with sportswriters before the fight that the only thing that kept him fit during this period of his life were the workouts he put himself through in order to train *me*. But once again, this time in the eighth round of a scheduled ten rounder, when Nova was having his way and turning Max's beautiful face to a bloody, swollen mess, the referee stopped the fight, and awarded the victory, by technical knockout, to Nova. This time nobody, Max included, disputed the decision.

In the dressing room afterwards, winking from a badly swollen left eye, and glancing down at his boxing trunks, Max declared he was still, at thirty-two, a young man whose working parts were in good order, and one with a wife and young son with whom he wished to spend more time. Because he didn't want to embarrass anyone again the way he had in the two fights against Nova—himself first of all—he was now going on record to announce that sportswriters and fight fans had just been witness to a major historical event: the last time anyone would ever see Max Baer enter the ring as a professional fighter.

The writers in attendance shouted out their disbelief and disapproval, but Max just grinned through a split upper lip, put his arm around me—I had already showered, and changed into street clothes—and said that his good friend here, who had suffered his first defeat in the ring—"He was robbed, guys," Max said, "and we all know it"—was the fighter to whom he would devote himself from now on.

"But that will not be possible," I said when reporters turned to me, "for like Max, I, too, am a young man with a wife and son I want to be with more consistently than a life in prize-fighting allows, and so, like my friend and mentor, on this night I, too, am hanging up my gloves."

This time Max made good on his promise. He never fought

professionally again (nor did I), although he would, to raise money for himself or charitable organizations, occasionally dance around the ring with another fighter in an exhibition, and when we spent time at the ranch in Livermore, we would sometimes spar with each other. And when we did, at *his* urging—in order that I be protected from what he called his "spontaneous eruptions"—I always wore headgear.

4　War

I opened to my beloved; but my beloved had withdrawn himself, and was gone: my soul failed when he spake: I sought him, but I could not find him; I called him, but he gave no answer. (5:6)

On January 7, 1942, one month after the Japanese attack on Pearl Harbor, Max enlisted in the army air corps. Although his official title was "athletic instructor," his main job was to go around the country selling war bonds, and he did this with his usual ebullience, telling cheering crowds that if we wanted to keep the world safe for our children and grandchildren, we had to all pull together to give those damned Nazis the licking they deserved. In many ways his military tour of duty turned out to be a three-year continuation, in uniform, of the life he'd been living: criss-crossing the country with actors, actresses, musicians, and fighters (including Buddy, who had enlisted with Max), and putting on exhibitions and performances (singing, dancing, acting, boxing, wrestling), and, as ever, clowning around in order to give himself *and* his audience a good time. There were differences, however: he did it all, he told the crowds, as a grateful employee trying to give his boss, Uncle Sam, a leg up on a world that was in trouble; and he did it, he said each time he took the stage, or entered a boxing ring, for a cause far greater than anything he had ever before fought for in his life.

Yet there was another difference: while he was going around the country for the army air corps, he and I were, for the first time since we had met on the night of Joleen's twenty-first birthday, separated from one another virtually all the time. He did come home every second or third month on official two- or three-day leaves, and when he was selling bonds on the west coast he would sometimes arrive in Sacramento (where we lived full-time through most of the war) for an overnight. But he spent his leaves and overnights with his family—Mary Ellen, Max Jr., Buddy, Augie, James Manny, and also, during the last year of the war, Maudie Marian, a daughter born to him and Mary Ellen in March 1944. And during these war years, to my knowledge, he and Joleen spent no time together except in the presence of others.

Three days after Max enlisted in the air corps, I went to the Port of Embarkation in Oakland (later named the Oakland Army Base) in the hopes of joining the navy. Although, like Max, I was eager to help defend our nation against its enemies, I did not own a birth certificate with either my given name (Joseph Barton), or the name of Horace Littlejohn on it, and so I asked Max if he would write me a letter of recommendation vouching for my date and place of birth (I told him that I was born on September 13, 1911, in Baton Rouge, Louisiana), my current place of residence, my years of service with him, my familial situation (wife and one child), and my reliability and good character.

Despite the esteem in which Max was held (at his urging, in addition to his letter of recommendation, I brought with me a folder containing newspaper clippings that told of my boxing career), and despite the armed forces' desperate need for able-bodied men, I was told there were, as yet, no places for colored men in the navy, army, or air corps units stationed at the Oakland facility. An officer, impressed with the letter from Max, assured me the situation was going to change; until it did, however, he recommended I make application to one of several all-Negro units being formed elsewhere in the country, or that I take a position as a civilian employee at the Oakland facility, where I could work either in the kitchens, or as a stevedore, loading and unloading supplies, equipment, and ammunition to and from ships stationed in the harbor.

Although, like many others, I might have been able to register for the draft without a valid birth certificate (or with one Max offered to have created for me), rather than risk the possible scrutiny such a ruse, if uncovered, might arouse (and thereby lead to revelations concerning my true relation to Joleen), I chose to take a civilian job as a stevedore, which job, given the dangers attached to the moving of large stores of ammunition, paid slightly more than a kitchen detail paid. In point of fact, several incidents would occur during the war wherein Negro soldiers, under pressure from their white officers to work with dispatch, were killed when ammunition they were loading onto ships exploded. One explosion, occurring less than an hour's drive from Oakland, at the Port Chicago facility near Martinez, resulted in the deaths of three hundred and twenty workers, virtually all of them Negro, and led to a mutiny by surviving Negro sailors who refused to continue loading ammunition under dangerous conditions. The result in this instance—the only case of a full military trial for mutiny in the history of the navy—was that these fifty Negro sailors were convicted, jailed, and given dishonorable discharges.

My own career at the Oakland base, though not without dangers—in my fourth month of work, I was put in charge of a unit of two dozen men specializing in the loading of ammunition on destroyers and aircraft carriers—proved less dramatic. I put in my time (often working sixty or more hours a week), received commendations, and was even—this in late 1943—encouraged by my commanding officer to join one of the few all-Negro units that were being granted permission to engage in combat operations. (Although more than two and a half million colored men registered for the draft during the war, only fifty thousand were permitted to serve in combat, this permission not granted until 1944.)

I chose to remain a stevedore. It was good, honorable work, and necessary to what proved, blessedly, a victorious cause. It also allowed me to help Joleen and Max's brother Augie keep the properties in Livermore and Sacramento in reasonably good repair. The only serious injury to any of us during the war years—and it was far from lethal—was to Max, who, while entertaining a group of soldiers, had an eighty-five pound punching bag fall on him, and do to him what no fighter had ever done: put him out of action. This happened late in 1944, a half year after Maudie Marion's birth, and resulted in disabling neck and shoulder injuries so that, with Italy having already surrendered (a substantial group of Italian prisoners of war worked at the Oakland Army Base, three of them assigned to my unit), and the wars in Europe and the Far East winding down, Max was given an honorable discharge and a special commendation for his exemplary service from both the commander in chief of the armed forces and the president of the United States.

During the years Max and Buddy were doing their part to help the United States and its allies prevail, and to bring about a peaceful accommodation between nations, however tainted and fraught with sorrow that peace may have been, Joleen and I also reached what I came to think of as a peaceful accommodation of our own, becoming to one another much like the married couple others believed we were. If at the time I had been able to put my sense of how Joleen and I got on with one another into words, I might have said that we had a loving understanding of the kind that informs those much-admired long-lasting marriages that persist in states of calm, contented companionship. We had, that is, friendship without rivalry, and intimacy without desire.

What made this possible, I believe, were not only habits we had acquired during our friendship with Max Baer, habits that had freed us in large degree from the desire to be physically intimate with one another, but—more—the happiness we found in being parents to Horace Jr., whose presence brought with it those sweet and ordinary responsibilities that, during years when we had seen no future for us other than the childless life we had with one another (and with Max Baer), we had come to believe would never be ours.

But just as the Lord gave a child to Abraham's wife, Sarah, when she had lived well past her childbearing years (so unexpected was the news that she was with child, the Bible tells us, that it made Sarah laugh), and did this not long after Abraham had informed King Abimelech that Sarah was his sister—just so had we been blessed with a child of our own when we had given up hope that, together *or* apart, this would ever be. And although we continued to sleep in the same bed (as we had begun doing when we were children), and sometimes to lie in one another's arms (and to do so with Horace Jr., when he was an infant, nestled between us), yet did we seem rarely if ever to have been tempted to renew with one another the act that had led to the life that was ours together.

Yet how curious, it occurs to me now, that we seemed so old when we were so young—more like an elderly aunt and uncle to

Horace Jr. than his parents—and how curious, too, that more than three score years after Horace Jr.'s birth, and nearly a half century after Max Baer's passing from this world, it often seems that we had never, with each other, done what we had done.

If I so choose, however, I *can* conjure up in detail not only the first time Joleen and I made love, but many other times after that. I have indulged this ability on occasion through the years (and somewhat more often in the period when I became aware I was losing my sight), and I have done so, in part, in order that, in the darkness in which I have increasingly come to live, I might confirm for myself that the life I believed I had was in fact the life I did have. And when I revisit these times, it is as if I am a ghost-like intruder watching someone else do what I did once upon a time.

Whereas ordinary sensory experiences—the scent of a rose, the sound of waves crashing on rocks, the taste of ripe raspberries, the sight (when sight was mine) of a storm-tossed sky, the feel of sandpaper or smooth stones upon my fingertips—can set in motion an unending sequence of feelings and desires—of associations, memories, and fantasies that seem as real as the world I inhabit, when it comes to Joleen—to feeling her hand on mine, or inhaling the almond-scented fragrance of her skin, or listening to her voice read to me from Scripture—all of which fill me, as ever, with pleasure, and send my mind tumbling through tunnels of memory—I can never recall our intimacy in any *corporeal* way. I can *see* us doing what we did, but I neither feel it happening again, nor does the memory of what happened lead to other feelings or memories.

Horace Jr. has often expressed gratitude to me for bequeathing to him the gift of memory that has been mine from my earliest years, which gift he has always claimed, no matter the truth of his lineage, to be his inheritance from me. Horace's memory is most acute when it comes to words on a page; once he has seen a phrase or a page he chooses to remember, he is capable of being able to retrieve that phrase or page at will. My own memory—like Horace's, lodged primarily in things visual—is more adept at recalling people, places, and objects, and, from the seemingly endless multitude of rooms housed in my many-chambered mind, to bring them forward into the light of day, as it were, and see them again in the fullness of who and what they once were.

It is possible, of course, that this is merely a way I have found to protect myself from feelings I feared might destroy me as they nearly destroyed Joleen, and it is also possible that my forthrightness in here recounting what happened is a way of denying its power over me, as in: it happened to me, yes, but so distant am I from what happened—so clearly do I see it—that it is as if I was not truly there. Whatever the explanation for the singular quality of my memory in this instance, I find that I cherish what did happen in a way not unlike the way I cherish Joleen and our love for one another. Not for us the more predictable and ordinary lives we, and Max, might have had had we never known one another.

What also remains curious is that when I recall our youthful love, and the extended moment in which it came into being, I find that I am increasingly put in mind of Joleen's tale of her brother James, and of her vengeance on his behalf. And when I imagine again what, in her tale, happened to James and to our father, I begin to think of James as if he, and not I, were brother to Joleen: as if his life were real in a way my own never was.

When I do—when I imagine James defending Joleen against our father, and imagine her lifting the jar of lye from under the pecan tree, I see something that actually did happen: I see Joleen lying under that same pecan tree, and I see myself coming upon her on the day when everything in our lives changed forever.

The sun was gone from the sky on what had been a brutally hot day in late August, and returning home from the fields, I saw that Joleen was by herself, her back against the pecan tree, and that she seemed to be in the midst of the kind of frightened, dream-tossed sleep that, in the bed we shared with our brother Paul, frequently plagued her. As I drew closer, I saw that her skirt, the deep black-brown of river-bottom, was raised above her waist. Her eyes were closed, and she had one hand between her legs while her other hand was pressed against her mouth in order, it seemed, to stifle growling sounds much like those our dogs would make when a person unknown to us came near.

I stopped and watched for a while, then approached as quietly as I could. As soon as I sat on the ground some eight to ten feet from her, however, she opened her eyes and smiled at me in a way that showed me she was not, as I feared, in pain. When she looked downwards as if, with her eyes, urging me to do the same, I saw that she wore no undergarment, and that her fingers were appearing and disappearing from view, then moving more and more quickly until, hunched over in what seemed a sudden seizure—her feet rising from the ground, her toes straightening—she let out a long, high-pitched sound that made me rush to her.

She collapsed against me, and held me close while strange whimpering sounds came from her throat. She touched my lips with her hand, and when she forced her fingers into my mouth and I tried to pull away, she took her hand from my mouth, dug her fingernails into my neck and, her mouth at my ear, whispered that I need not be frightened—"I'm all right, so don't be frightened, brother," she said. "I'm all right, so don't be frightened"—and that I should please, please hold her as tightly as I could.

I did what she asked. The back of her thin shirt was wet through, while her skin was slick with sweat. When, several minutes later, she let out a long exhalation of air, leaned back, and shook her head up and down several times to indicate that she *was* all right, I asked her what she had been doing that had brought on such spasms.

"Oh my dear brother," she said, "I have just been to the moon."

"I do not understand," I said.

She placed two fingers against my mouth, and this time, though their scent and taste were, as before, rank, they possessed a sweetness that made me want to take them into *my* mouth. Before I could, however, she pushed me away, and let her hand rest again between her thighs.

"This is what happened," she said. "When I delivered laundry to the Cogswell family this afternoon, the young woman with whom I converse from time to time—Margaret Jane—met me at the door, showed me where to put the laundry, paid me, and asked if I would care to join her and her brother for tea.

"I said that it was not possible for me to accept such an invitation, but she told me she and her brother were alone in the house. Her brother appeared then, and he was to her as you are to me, two years younger, while Margaret Jane—I knew this from previous conversations—was but eight or nine months older than I am. Fearful she would take my refusal as insolence, and hearing no sounds indicating there were other people about, when she again insisted I join them—'I expect you to do what I ask,' were her words—I let her lead me to a veranda at the rear of the house that was screened in, its shades let down, and I sat where she told me to sit.

"Then she lay down on a divan, and after a while she lifted her skirt, and when I saw that she wore nothing below the skirt, I covered my eyes and stood, but her brother pried my hand from my eyes, pushed me back into my chair, and sat beside me. He did not touch me again. Instead, while his sister began to move her fingers in and out of herself, he put his own hand inside his trousers.

"Margaret Jane kept smiling at me, but her smile was forced and the laughter that accompanied it shrill, as if she were on the verge of hysterics. At the same time, despite the fact that I remained mute, she kept asking if I had ever done what she was doing, and so astonished was I by what was happening that it was all I could do to shake my head sideways, and look about, frightened to death someone would find me with them, and that my punishment for being there would in fact *become* the death of me.

"A moment later her brother, eyes closed, shuddered and let his head fall backwards. He was soon asleep, a doltish smile on his face, and while he slept, Margaret Jane ordered me to do what she was doing, and said that if I did her bidding there might be a reward, but that if I did *not* do what she said . . ."

"Dear Joleen—how awful!" I exclaimed.

"Not at all," Joleen said. "Oh not at all, for when I did what she told me to do, I experienced sensations that, though familiar, opened this time into sensations I did not know I could have, and when these sensations led to an explosion within me, like a rush of brilliant stars crashing down with a great and mighty roar, I also found myself floating happily in the air above myself, and then Margaret Jane closed her eyes, and went into mild convulsions that, I am certain, she knew were not in their intensity anything like mine. And was that not the greatest pleasure of all, to have outdone her at her own beloved game? For I was on my way to the moon, and when I returned, I was able, while Margaret Jane, her mouth agape, watched in awe, to send myself there again, and again, and again.

"And now," she said, "the sun having set and the moon rising, you may accompany me while I travel there once more . . ."

This was when she saw that I had, listening to her tale, become aroused, and she reached out to touch me—I backed away at once—and said that Margaret Jane had told her that sometimes her brother did for her what she had been doing for herself, and that Margaret

Jane did not know how she could have survived the endless *ennui* of her life—"oh the boredom, the terrible boredom and *ennui!*" she cried—had they not played such games with one another.

"I did not believe her," Joleen said. "But I believe that if you really love me the way you say you do, you will do with me now what Margaret Jane claims she and her brother do with and for one another."

I scuttled backwards on the ground, but Joleen was upon me at once, tugging on the thin cloth of my trousers, and asking again, if I really, *really* loved her, why would I not do what she asked, for it was a simple thing no one would ever know about, and that—was this what vanquished the last, frail vestige of my resistance?—even the great patriarchs and matriarchs of the Bible, along with their children, had done with one another.

5

Enchanted Hills

*Awake. O north wind; and come, thou
south; blow upon my garden, that the
spices thereof may flow out. Let my
beloved come into his garden, and eat his
pleasant fruits. (4:16)*

Although, when Max and I were on
tour together after the war, just the two of us, and he was either
performing vaudeville routines, or working as a celebrity referee, we
resumed our intimacies, we did so with decreasing frequency, and
without anything like the passion that had informed our earlier
times together. Whether this was due to the hiatus in our liaisons
necessitated by the war, or to Max's taking his familial responsibilities more seriously now that he was a father of three, or to a
certain calming effect on my emotions that came as a result of the
accommodation Joleen and I had reached, or simply to the passage
of time, I cannot say. But it soon became clear in these post-war

years that Max and I had become to one another good friends and companions in much the way Joleen and I had, and though this transformation was unanticipated and, at first, disheartening, it was not unpleasant.

During the telling of my story, as during the nearly four decades that have passed since Max Baer's death, in November of 1959, I have frequently found myself wondering how it could be that so much sheer and abundant energy was gone from the world, and— more!—how it could be that Joleen and I had lived on together after Max's passing for more years than those in which we knew him. Having set out to tell the story of the Max Baer I knew, and of the life I knew with him, at a time when my own physical well-being was in decline, I am surprised to find, as I draw near to the end of the task, that I have gained strength from the journey. It has given me great and unexpected pleasure to be able to put my memories into words, to remember experiences as if they occurred no more than a few weeks ago, and to be able to conjure up, in addition, experiences I dimly recalled, or recalled not at all until the moment I began to recount what I *did* remember.

Thus, while the strength I have gained from the task remains, I will set down one more story—a story with distinctly *un*pleasant elements, and a story I have kept to myself for nearly half a century. It may be that Joleen will judge this a story that should go to the grave with me. It is my hope, however, that she will write down what I here reveal, and it is my wish that our son, Horace Jr., thereby learn of what happened, and that it be left to him to decide whether the events I describe, as with those ancient manuscripts he ponders, are worthy of being preserved.

In the early summer of 1958, about a year before Max's death, and Horace Jr.'s graduation from the University of California at

Berkeley, I became aware that my eyesight was failing. At this time, Joleen and I were living in a house of our own in San Francisco, a house built into the side of a hill where, from our second-floor bedroom—our *only* room on the second floor—we could see, through the open spaces between homes that lay, on descending levels between our house and the Embarcadero, a vertical slice of San Francisco Bay and, rising up above it, the magnificent Golden Gate Bridge, a bridge that did not exist when we had first come to San Francisco. Our house was situated in a neighborhood that had, for most of this century, been largely Italian, but was now quite diverse. In addition to a scattering of black families and, still, a fair number of Italians, mostly elderly, there was a large population of Asians—Chinese, Japanese, and Korean—as well as substantial communities of Russians, Mexicans, and college-educated white families with young children.

Our home, built in 1916, was a simple, solid clapboard house with lovely Wedgewood-blue trim and shutters, and it suited us well. Without a basement, it had a galley kitchen and combination dining area and living room on the first floor, where Horace Jr. slept on a daybed when he was home from college, and, on the second floor, adjoining the bedroom, a fair-sized storage area. There was a narrow, thin-walled mud room at the rear of the house, and a front porch that was ample, and upon which we often sat, especially in the late afternoon or early evening, reading, or watching the changing colors of the sky.

Our needs were modest, and we had solved the problem of where to keep the many books we had accumulated by donating a large quantity of them to our local library in San Francisco while retaining one or two books each by favorite authors, along with books that had sentimental value: Horace Jr.'s childhood books, scrapbooks that chronicled Max's boxing career (and mine), and—the largest single grouping, which we kept on wide floor-to-ceiling shelves that lined the lone doorless and windowless wall of our bedroom—religious books: several Bibles, picture books of Jerusalem and the Holy Land, and books about both the Hebrew and Christian Bibles that were especially meaningful to Joleen, for she believed they had been the inspiration for Horace Jr.'s choice of vocation, and had, during her dark times, nurtured in her qualities that had kept her mind and spirit from deteriorating.

During the decade that followed the war, Max had come to spend the greater portion of his time either in Hollywood, for the making of movies and commercials, or at home in Sacramento with Mary Ellen and their children. Although I usually accompanied him on trips that took him beyond the borders of California, and though he and I continued to spar now and then, it was clear that he had less and less need for my services. At the same time, their children no longer infants, Mary Ellen was able, with help from her mother, who came to live with us in 1953 (both of Max's parents had died before the war), to take care of the house and grounds without our assistance. Nor did she or Max ask for Joleen's assistance in tutoring their children.

When, in 1955, the Baers sold the ranch in Livermore, our presence in the Baer household became, in Joleen's words, decidedly redundant. It is my belief, too, though I do not know this for certain, that the decline of my intimacies with Max paralleled a similar decline in his intimacies with Joleen.

And so, one evening in the last week of July 1956, when Joleen and I had, after serving dinner to Max and his family, joined them for dessert and coffee as we were sometimes invited to do, Joleen used the occasion to announce that she had been to San Francisco the day before, and had begun a process for the renewal of her teacher's license. In order to qualify, though, she would be required to take two additional college-level courses, which she could do in the evenings. In the interim, she would obtain employment as a teacher's assistant. Within the next week or two, and in time for the opening of public schools after Labor Day, she could expect a provisional placement that the person who interviewed her at the offices of the board of education assured her would be forthcoming.

Ten days later, Joleen received notice of a position open to her in a school in the Mission Hill section of the city, a neighborhood that had been mostly Polish and Irish but was, more recently, becoming home to Mexican families, and she registered for the two courses she needed in order to update her credentials. At the same time, she and I began looking for a home of our own in San Francisco and, after we had found the one we came to live in and informed Max of our intention to make an offer for it, he told us that, in gratitude for the years of service we had given him and his family, he was going to bestow a gift of cash upon us that would enable us to buy the house outright.

We accepted his gift, and moved into the house in the fall of 1957, two weeks before the start of the school year. That same week Joleen received a letter of appointment to a position as a full-time fifth-grade teacher in an elementary school in the Mission Hill school where she had been working as a teacher's assistant. Nor had I been idle. At the beginning of the summer, I had taken a part-time position at the Granelli's Boxing Gym, performing janitorial tasks while also working with young fighters who trained there. One of them, a twenty-year-old Mexican named Luis Olmo Sanchez, a welterweight who had been a regional Golden Gloves finalist the previous year, told me that the Embarcadero YMCA that sponsored him was looking for someone to coach their boxing teams. He had already spoken to the director of the YMCA about me, and so I applied for the job and, my association with Max Baer and my own boxing career proving valuable assets, I was offered a full-time position wherein my responsibilities would be divided between being assistant youth activities director, and coach of the YMCA's two traveling teams: one for boys above the age of sixteen, and the other, a "Silver Gloves" team, for boys between the ages of ten and fifteen.

The YMCA was located on Fillmore Street, a convenient ten- or twelve-minute walk from our house. I enjoyed scheduling youth activities within the YMCA—basketball leagues, swim meets, workout schedules, skill classes, and exercise classes—but my great pleasure lay in training and coaching the boxing teams. When the director of the YMCA put up a notice on the bulletin board in the building's lobby about me joining "the YMCA family," and also succeeded in getting an article in the Sunday edition of the *San Francisco Chronicle* about me—about my career with Max, and my own stint in the boxing world—a two-page spread with pictures, and the announcement that for those unable to afford membership for their children, there would be a dozen scholarships made available to worthy boys and young men, we were overwhelmed with applicants. The scholarships were named in memory of Frankie Campbell, who, I had learned from the director of the YMCA, had been a member of the YMCA's traveling team and a national Golden Gloves light-heavyweight champion a year before he turned professional. The scholarships had been endowed, anonymously, by Max.

I invited Max to meet with my teams, which he did several times, and when he did, to the delight of everyone at the YMCA, he put on great shows: telling jokes, reminiscing about his fights, giving the boys pointers, especially about footwork, which he would introduce by performing brief tap dances that had us all handclapping. He would also spar with me, and all the while we traded jabs, feints, and punches he would chatter away about what he was doing and why, and about how lucky everyone was to have a great boxer like me as their coach.

I also continued, though at greater intervals, to accompany him to some of his out-of-town engagements, which usually took place on weekends, though if one of his engagements required that I be away from the YMCA for a day or two during the week, grateful for the publicity generated by Max's visits (and for his generous donations to the scholarship fund), the YMCA would grant me time off to be with him.

The stated mission of the Golden Gloves of America, posted on a wall of a large room the YMCA put aside for the use of our teams, was to provide an active and safe environment that protected and enhanced the physical and emotional well-being and social development of young men by developing their athletic skills, sense of good sportsmanship, self-respect, work ethic, and pride, while also providing wholesome entertainment for the community. The possibility that any of the young men I worked with would become professional prizefighters was minimal, and so I devoted myself to inculcating in them a sense of self-discipline—a work ethic they could apply to other realms of their lives—and to perfecting their defensive skills, which could, in those chance encounters that might occur throughout their lives, prove useful in insuring their safety, as well as the safety of others.

Within a few months, improvements in the skill levels of the boys were such that, after doing well in local tournaments against teams sponsored by the police and fire departments, we entered our first regional event. It took place an hour away, in the Stanford University gymnasium (Stanford University did not itself officially sponsor a boxing team, but it did have a first-rate boxing "club" that included several members of their nationally ranked football team), and at this event we came away with two champions in the Silver Gloves categories, at weights of 135 and 160, and three Golden Gloves winners, at weights of 112, 118, and 160. The team was ecstatic, as were their families and the larger YMCA community, and we received excellent press in both the *San Francisco Chronicle* and the *San Francisco Examiner.*

I never sparred with boxers on our teams, but I would shadow-box alongside them, and I'd put on punch mitts and have them go at me, and—how I came to acknowledge the degree to which my eyesight had been failing—one afternoon in April I challenged our best heavyweight, a young Negro boy named Billy Pidgeon (he had been defeated at Stanford by a young man who would go on to become an All-American linebacker), to throw everything he had at me. He did so with enthusiasm and, while drilling me with lefts and rights in patterns I had taught him—one two slip; two two slip; one two one two slip slip; one two one two slip slip slip—he suddenly faked a left to my right mitt, and swung a roundhouse right that caught me by surprise and hit me so hard on the side of my head—I was not wearing protective headgear—that, though I did not fall, I became aware, immediately, of a dead cushion of air to the right of me that meant I had lost hearing there.

To my relief, my hearing returned several minutes later. Billy apologized, insisting he had not meant to hurt me but had been carried away by my command to give me all he had, and while members of our team gathered around, I praised Billy for the strength and swiftness of his blow, but reminded him that power without discipline was as useless as discipline without power. I urged him to stick to the routines, and only the routines, until he was ready to go it on his own in a free-style manner informed by what he did not yet possess: a sure knowledge of essentials and, equally important, control *of* those essentials.

On my walk home that day, I realized that, though my hearing seemed fine, my vision was not. I was squinting in order to see things—boats in the bay, cars along the highway leading to the bridge, signs on storefronts—and, at times, though not in a consistent manner, I was repeating a habit that had, in recent months, become second nature: turning my head slightly to the right or to the left in the hope this would enable me to see things directly in my line of vision more clearly. Had Billy's blow dislodged something critical to my vision, I wondered—a temporary loss such as those I had suffered in earlier years during and after several bouts—or had his blow aggravated a condition that had been there, on and off, for nearly a year but that I had been choosing to ignore?

Two days later, when Joleen and I were sitting on our front porch after dinner—it had rained heavily the night before and into the early afternoon, and the air seemed to have been vacuumed clean so that when one stood at the far end of our porch, one could see farther than ever into the Bay and across the Bay to Marin County, to the sailboats anchored there, and to the houses on low rising hills beyond—I told her about the blow I had taken to the head, and also about my vision—that objects in front of me had been becoming more and more severely blurred, as if smudged, with each passing day.

Rather than chastise me for having kept this information from her, she put me through some simple tests: standing first to one side of me and then to the other, and moving several steps backwards and forward while I kept my eyes fixed on a point in front of me so that we could determine when I began to lose sight of her. When we had established that my peripheral vision had not been compromised in a significant way, Joleen had me compare what she could see at various distances—a particular boat at rest along the Embarcadero shoreline, or moving out to sea, a chimney or television antenna on a nearby rooftop—and the results led her to an obvious conclusion: I should make an appointment to see our family doctor as soon as possible.

"Not an eye doctor?" I said.

"Not an eye doctor," she said, and she said no more, but it was clear she already suspected my failing eyesight was a result, not of an accumulation of blows to the head, or to a loss of vision that might normally accompany aging (Joleen had begun wearing eyeglasses several years before), but was a consequence of something more commonly lethal, especially, as I would learn, for Negro men: diabetes.

Our family physician, Doctor Martin Baskin, gave me a thoroughgoing examination. After the examination, he asked me when I had last seen an eye doctor, and I replied that I had *never* been to an eye doctor because I had never, until recent months, experienced any problems with my eyesight. He said he was going to refer me to a colleague, Doctor Simeon Levitzky, an ophthalmologist, and expected Doctor Levitzky to concur with the preliminary diagnosis he had arrived at: that my problems with vision were caused by diabetes.

He made this diagnosis not only because of the significant loss of visual acuity shown by my difficulties in reading an eye chart, but because of what he saw when he looked into my eyes with his ophthalmoscope: the presence of apparently new and fragile blood vessels covering the surface of the clear, vitreous gel that filled the visible part of the eye. He expected that Doctor Levitzky would find similar blood vessels growing *within* the eye, along the retina, that some of the blood vessels would be found to have been leaking blood—hemorrhaging—and that it was this ongoing process that was causing vision loss and could eventually lead to blindness.

This initial diagnosis was based on several other factors: my telling him that I had been losing weight though I had not changed my diet in any way, and my report of symptoms that commonly accompanied the onset of diabetes: increased appetite and thirst, and greater frequency of urination. He predicted that when results from blood tests arrived, they would show high levels of blood sugar, and that this would be an indication that my body either was not producing enough insulin, or that it was not able to metabolize the insulin being produced. In addition—what had informed Joleen's diagnosis—diabetes was a disease with a higher than average prevalence among Negro men, and occurred with increasing frequency as Negro men aged.

I saw Doctor Levitzky two days later, and he confirmed Doctor Baskin's diagnosis. I had diabetic retinopathy, and had, he believed, been suffering from it for some time. The fact that I had failed to inform Joleen or anyone else about my blurred vision or—another telltale symptom I had been ignoring—the persistent flights across my line of vision of red specks (blood!) had not been helpful, and only the fact that I had remained fit, and had not gained excessive weight (and had not, thus, driven my blood sugar to even higher levels), had kept my condition from becoming worse. At the same time, however, being in excellent physical shape had masked the gravity of my condition, and had kept me from acknowledging that there was cause for alarm.

To complicate an already grave situation, Doctor Levitzky concluded I was also suffering from what was called macular edema, which resulted when fluid created by abnormal blood vessels, along with fatty deposits, leaked into the center of the macula—the part of the eye responsible for straight-ahead vision. Alas, he said, macula edema was rarely reversible.

The prospects, he said, both literally and figuratively, were not—apt word—bright. There were no surgical treatments he trusted that were capable of reversing what was happening. It was his opinion that cauterization, for example, which some ophthalmologists might recommend, would do more harm than good (laser surgery was still decades away), though he thought insulin could slow down the course of the diabetes. He suggested that Joleen and I come in together so that his nurse could teach us how to administer injections. He prescribed a minimal daily dosage that he would increase gradually as needed, and as my condition became more grave.

The most important advice he could give me, however, was to prepare for the possibility that my loss of vision would be progressive and that I might, within a few years, lose my eyesight entirely. "By vocation and character," he said then, "you are a fighter, Mister Littlejohn. But against the natural course of illness and disease, being a fighter who battles an adversary has little relevance for a condition such as yours."

He strongly advised that I do no boxing whatsoever, and that I limit weight lifting and other exercises that might prove jarring to my system and could thereby induce hemorrhaging. Most of all, he urged me to visit the offices of the San Francisco Lighthouse for the Blind in order to educate myself about future eventualities.

And then—this was the first and only time this rather severe man, whose mien was itself defined by the very word he repeatedly used to describe my situation—"grave"—smiled at me. He wanted me to be sure that the person I saw at the Lighthouse for the Blind was Miss Marie-Anne Hémon, to whom he had previously referred several patients. She was highly knowledgeable about services available to individuals with vision loss, and this was due in part to the fact that she was herself the mother of a boy who suffered from a significant visual impairment. In addition, she had a daughter who, though not completely deaf, suffered from substantial hearing loss.

He believed these unhappy facts of her life enabled her to be unusually empathic to the people with whom she worked. She was, also, a woman of color, and he thought this fact would put me at ease when I conferred with her about my condition.

Joleen accompanied me to the doctor's office the next day, and on the following day she began administering the insulin injections. Two days after that, I began administering them myself. That week I was also fitted for eyeglasses, which helped enormously, and which, when I wore them to the YMCA, caused many comments and much teasing. Although I did not inform anyone there of the seriousness of my condition, I did reduce my levels of physical activity, and when a member of my teams would ask why I was doing so, I would simply make use of the old line about my adversaries surely not wanting to hit a man who wore glasses. I also said I believed in granting my young boxers the increasing autonomy that came with their growing mastery of the skills I had been endeavoring to teach them.

The boys sometimes laughed among themselves at what they thought of as my old-fashioned way of expressing things, and in this they were no different, of course, than Max had been at the start of our friendship, and so I took to exaggerating my fanciful use of language in order that they would continue to laugh at me and, thus, not suspect the real reasons for my diminishing involvement in their workouts.

A week after I had begun daily injections, I took the Market Street Cable Car to the city's civic center, and walked from there to the building on Van Ness Street that housed the San Francisco Lighthouse for the Blind. A few minutes after I told the receptionist that I had a one o'clock appointment with Miss Marie-Anne Hémon, a tall, youthful-looking woman whose skin was of a color we had, in

Louisiana, and not in a flattering way, called high yellow, came toward me, extending her hand and saying, warmly, but with a mischievous sparkle in her eyes, "You must be the famous—or shall I say *in*famous—Horace Littlejohn." I shook her hand, and affirmed that I was one and the same, and it was in that swiftly passing moment that I sensed—that I *knew*—my life was about to change as profoundly as it had on the evening nearly three decades before when Max Baer had first taken my hand in his.

Miss Hémon led me upstairs to her second-floor office, chatting with me all the way, telling me of the letter she had received from Doctor Levitzky, and about how she had gone to her local library— she lived in the Portero Hill section of town, not far from the school in the Mission Hill section where Joleen taught—and found newspaper articles about me and my work at the YMCA.

She also told me she had mentioned that I would be coming in for an interview to one of the men who worked as a porter at the Lighthouse, and whom she knew to be an avid boxing fan. Hawkins Johnson was his name—he had come to the Lighthouse four years before, after he had lost the use of his left eye—and she said he claimed to have seen me fight several times, and also to have seen me at some of Max Baer's fights when I was working with Max.

He was counting on me to arrange a meeting for him with Max Baer himself. Hawkins was not, Miss Hémon noted, known for his shyness. In fact, he had knocked on her door earlier in the day, said he remembered that today would be the day I would be there, and reminded her that she had promised to introduce him to me. She then asked if it was true, as both Hawkins Johnson and the newspaper articles maintained, that I had been an exceptionally gifted boxer, and I replied that I had been, perhaps, a bit more than merely competent, and I deflected more talk about my career by talking about Max Baer, and about what it had been like to be with him before and after he became heavyweight champion of the world.

I went on to explain that my wife and I had met Max Baer while celebrating her twenty-first birthday, and that we had served him and his family faithfully for many years, and when I mentioned that his son and mine had been born less than six months apart, and had become great good friends, she asked me to tell her about Horace Jr., which I did, after which I asked her about her children, prefacing my question by noting that Doctor Levitzky had told me of their handicaps, and saying that if she preferred not to talk about them, I would understand. But she scoffed at my politeness, and said she felt herself doubly blessed—that her children were the jewels and miracles of her life—and we were off and flying then, trading stories about our children—she, too, it turned out, had once upon a time believed she would go through life without ever having a child of her own—and of what a great joy it was to see them grow and change. She told me, for example, about her daughter's first day of kindergarten. The son, not yet in school, was seventeen months younger than the daughter, and had sulked most of the morning. When Miss Hémon asked him what was bothering him, he had remained mute. Suspecting the source of the problem, Miss Hémon asked if he was missing his sister. Her son had replied that yes, he missed his sister, and then, looking up, added: "But don't tell her. Please?"

We also found ourselves talking of the frustrations that accompanied parenting—of our hopes for our children and, more, of our fears *for* our children. We talked about how it often seemed that in the end it all came down to nothing more—or less—than love and worry. The next thing I knew, she was glancing at her watch and informing me that nearly an hour had passed since my arrival, and that she had to leave in order to be home for her children. She apologized for not having introduced me to Hawkins Johnson, for not having given me a tour of the facility, or even—hadn't this been the reason for my visit?—talked with me about the services the Lighthouse offered. Would I promise to return very soon so that— and here I sensed she was playfully mocking my decorous manner of speech—she might make proper amends and correct her errant ways?

I said I would welcome the opportunity, and when she suggested I return on the following Monday I said that I held meetings with my teams beginning at half-past three each Monday afternoon to discuss their training schedules for the coming week.

"Well then, Mister Littlejohn," she said, "why don't you see what you can do to rearrange your schedule so that we might continue our conversation. That is what our work here is about, after all, and we shouldn't lose sight of it, wouldn't you agree?"

She added that I need not respond to the antic and silly mood that unexpectedly, as now, often rose up within her. Saying this, she shook my hand, and led me to the door, and when she did I recalled two things I had noticed in the first moment I had looked upon her face—what, without eyeglasses, I might not have noticed: that though her coloring was far lighter than Joleen's, she had put me in mind of what Joleen had looked like as a young woman. She was not, perhaps, as striking-looking as Joleen had been: she was more pretty than beautiful, more ordinary and plain than unusual or mysterious, yet she bore an uncanny resemblance to Joleen in the way a lighter-skinned younger sister might have resembled an older sister. And my eyes had been drawn, too, to her wide-set brown eyes and cheekbones, which were not quite as wide-set as Joleen's, and to her mouth—to her full, plum-colored lips, and to a pale, thin vertical scar, perhaps a half inch in length, at the left corner of her lower lip and of how, when she smiled, the scar seemed to spread slightly, and to glisten in the way a leaf might when covered with a skin of morning dew. I wanted to touch the scar—to ask her how and why it was there—but instead I took the hand she extended, and said that unless she heard otherwise from me, I would look forward to seeing her at noon on Monday.

After Miss Hémon and I had exchanged perfunctory greetings about being pleased to see each other again, and she had informed me that she had written out a schedule for our visit, she leaned forward on her desk, her chin propped on clasped hands, and asked, pointedly, "Are you all *right*, Mister Littlejohn?"—to which I responded by asking her why she asked such a question, to which she, with a half smile, said that she asked it for no reason other than the fact that my hands were trembling, and my forehead and upper lip were beaded with sweat.

I patted my forehead and upper lip with a handkerchief, and then, without regard to consequences, I spoke.

"Yes," I said, "I am all right, but sitting here and seeing you again, I *am* somewhat unnerved, for I am struck again, as I was during our meeting last week, by the fact that although there are significant differences, yet you do bear a remarkable resemblance to what my wife, Joleen, looked like when she was a young woman of your age."

"And what age do you imagine that to be?" Miss Hémon asked.

"Although I do not know the ages of your children, which would allow me to give a more accurate estimate, I would guess that you are in your middle or late twenties."

"Ah, Mister Littlejohn," she said, sitting back in her chair. "You are trying to get into my good graces by flattery. Or perhaps you are merely doing what many men do when they wish to find favor in a woman's eyes: telling her she is much younger than they know her to be."

"Not at all," I said quickly. "Oh not at all, Miss Hémon. Please believe me. If anything—if not for the fact that you told me you are mother to two children—if I had not known this fact, that is—I would have taken you for a woman in her *early* twenties."

"I am thirty-eight years old," she said.

"I am astonished," I said. "And I must wonder how it is that you have such an unworried and youthful appearance."

"Suffering," she said.

"Suffering?"

"Yes, suffering, which when translated into the quotidian matter of my workaday life is interchangeable with responsibilities. Now *there's* a word we might chew on for a while, don't you think? For— to return your frankness with my own—it has been my *responsibilities*, I believe, especially for my children, that have kept me young, though not, as you would have it, *unworried.*" Then, before I could respond, she continued. "But look—just look at me, will you, please? Or rather, since you have clearly spent more than sufficient time doing that—*listen* to me! *Listen* to how I am talking!"

"To how you are you *talking?*" I said. "I don't understand. You talk with great clarity—you are an exceptionally articulate woman."

"How I am talking," she laughed. "Why I am talking like *you*, Mister Littlejohn! I am using your most proper locutions as if I did so on a regular basis, and do you know what?"

"I do not."

"I enjoy doing so," she said. "I am what we call, in our practices, *mirroring you*, and isn't that a wonder—that I am able to talk in this way, and how, pray tell—please, Mister Littlejohn—how pray tell am I doing so, and *why* am I doing so, and—more important— how did you come to speak in the way *you* do?"

Though both disarmed and enchanted by her directness, I responded in a calm and measured way. "It is a gift from my wife,

Joleen, and to the two of us from the Holy Bible," I explained. "For we often read from it to one another, and having led a somewhat isolated life—insular, one might say, for my wife and I have spent more time with one another, and with our son, than with others, with the exception, of course, of the time I spent traveling with Max Baer—we developed the habit, without knowing it *was* a habit, of talking with one another in the way people in the Bible talk. And . . ."

"And what?"

". . . and until this moment I had never articulated in words how my manner of speaking—and of thinking, for that matter—came to be."

"And mannered it surely is," she said. "And how *wonderful* that it is, and that you and your wife have made your life with one another—your marriage—so unique by the *manner* of your communication."

"Yes," I said. "Thank you."

We sat in silence for a while, and then, softly, she spoke the very words I had been thinking but had not felt brave enough to express aloud.

"We are going to be good friends, I expect, aren't we?" she said.

"I hope so," I said.

"But I also expect to help you in the journey you have begun— a journey that will enable you to see the world, its people and wonders—and its darkness, too, for sure—when your eyes may no longer be of assistance to you *on* your journey. So let me explain what services we offer for people of limited vision here—services we hope you will not need for some time, and let me also inform you of the more complete range of services we can offer if and when your vision does decline significantly."

I nodded my assent, after which she led me on a tour of the

building. We started in the library, on the ground floor, where she introduced me to the head librarian, Miss Florence Duncan, a stout lady with voluminous braids of white hair held in place atop her head with ornaments and pins. An assortment of some half dozen necklaces—strands of pearls and strings of what appeared to be precious stones—hung around her neck and rested on an exceptionally ample bosom. She had several items in readiness for my arrival—large-print books, books printed in Braille, and books about learning how to read Braille. She showed me a microfilm reader that would be available to me, and how to operate it so as to enlarge texts I would see on its screen. She provided me with pamphlets about the library's contents and use—in print, and in Braille—and a brochure about the classes in learning to read Braille that the Lighthouse offered. To virtually every presentation and explanation she made, she would add: "Do you see what I mean, Mister Littlejohn?"

She also showed me a short film about the history of the San Francisco Lighthouse for the Blind, which, I learned, had been founded in 1902, and had been housed originally in the basement of San Francisco's main library. Shortly before the First World War it acquired a home of its own—it had since moved again, to its present location—and had been renowned, as it still was, for its "blind-craft": the production, by its blind members, of brooms, baskets, and, more recently, furniture.

She showed me where I would find boxes of alphabet cards I could employ for practicing my skills at reading Braille, and she showed me Braille typewriters, and slates and styluses used for writing Braille by hand. She introduced me to her assistants-in-training, Pamela and Gail, both of whom were blind. They were, she laughed, "star *pupils* in her eyes," and these two individuals, whom I judged to be in their early thirties, performed for me: reading aloud passages from the Bible—I recognized them as being from The Book of Daniel—while running their fingers along embossed dots on sheets of Braille script. They typed out words on Braille typewriters, and they wrote, in Braille, on their slates, and on paper, and when one of them turned over a page the other had written, and skimmed the surface of the page with her fingertips, she was able to translate the newly formed dots into words that—she gave me the sheet of paper to keep as a souvenir of my visit—warmly welcomed Mister Horace Littlejohn to the San Francisco Lighthouse for the Blind.

I suppose I should have been cheered by their skillfulness—by the knowledge that, even were I to become blind, I would still be able to read and, as I would learn from others Miss Hémon introduced me to that day, to get along in the world with reasonable efficiency—but though outwardly I voiced gratitude, inwardly I felt lost.

Miss Hémon took my arm, and led me from the library even while thanking Miss Duncan and her assistants, and apologizing to them for our hasty exit. She said there were others waiting to meet with us, and in the way she turned me toward the door, I felt as if she were already guiding a blind person toward an unseen destination. Did she sense my unease? My sorrow? Could she have known, despite my outward demeanor, or *because* of it, how sad I felt to be there, and to be contemplating a life wherein I would one day have to imagine the world into being? Could she hear the ragged tumblings of my soul, or sense the strange tightening I felt in my chest?

Miss Hémon next introduced me to Richard Ratner, program director of the Lighthouse—one of the few individuals on staff who, like her, had normal vision—and who talked about programs the Lighthouse offered: Braille classes, of course, and also cooking classes, classes devoted to home safety and daily living skills, as well as to transportation, travel, and employment. We then left the main building, where, as if leading us around a movie studio lot, he took us into an annex—a cottage containing several rooms, in which rooms, including a kitchen with ingeniously designed utensils and appliances, Lighthouse members could learn to navigate safely on their own, and to perform domestic chores. He showed me pictures of Enchanted Hills Camp, a Lighthouse retreat of more than three hundred acres, near the city of Napa, where both visually and hearing impaired individuals could meet and socialize with others who shared their disabilities.

He ended his presentation by escorting us to the second-floor store, where Phillip Yarnell, the man in charge, expounded on various items that could be purchased: canes and cane tips, magnifying glasses, binoculars, slates and styluses, alphabet cards, watches whose clear plastic lids opened so you could read the time with your fingers, and books printed in Braille.

We then accompanied Mister Yarnell to the basement, and to the Lighthouse's pride and joy: its Blindcraft Center, where on this day some dozen or so men and women were working at tasks involved in the making of baskets, brooms, and furniture. There were three paid staff members working with them, and the room was filled with noise and chatter. Having enjoyed, through the years, repairing and constructing small items—bookcases, chairs, tables—for Joleen and myself, as well as helping in the physical maintenance of the Baer household and ranch—I found myself waking from my despondent state. I watched two sightless men, in carpenter's overalls, on a raised platform in the room's center, joining together the parts of a large table. I introduced myself to the men, said that the table was more than admirable, and that, perhaps—I said this so they would understand I was knowledgeable enough to appreciate the quality of their work—when a stain had been applied, and a preservative coat of oil, shellac, or wax, I would return so that—we laughed at my choice of words—I could see it in its *finished* incarnation.

Miss Hémon next suggested we adjourn to the building's cafeteria, located adjacent to the Blindcraft Center. We had just seated ourselves at a table—past lunch hour, the room was deserted—when a tall, lean, elderly Negro man, limping slightly, a red paisley bandana on his head and a black eye patch over his left eye, approached us.

"You're Horace Littlejohn, ain't you?" he said, and he put out his hand.

"This is Hawkins Johnson," Miss Hémon said. "Hawkins, this is Mister Horace Littlejohn."

"I am pleased to meet you," I said, and then, instead of shaking my hand, Hawkins took the fingers of my right hand in his.

"This man gonna be good at reading the Braille," he said. "I know this man, see—oh I know him good. Ain't nobody ever seen these fingers forget this man. 'Frank "long-fingered" Joleen Jr.' they called him, in memory of the man *your* man put in the ground by that wicked right hand of his . . ."

I said that Miss Hémon had talked favorably about him, but he waved away my remark, and, his mouth close to my face, he suddenly seized the back of my neck. He seemed to have no teeth, and his breath reeked of chewing tobacco—I could see a large plug of it wedged between his gums and his cheek, though how he would be able to chew tobacco without teeth was puzzling—and for a moment, so forceful was his grip on my neck, and so close his mouth to my cheek, I feared he was going either to kiss me, or—strange thought—to *bite* me.

"So listen, my brother," he said, letting go of me. "When you gonna let me meet the great man himself, Mister Maximilian Baer?"

"Perhaps," I began, "you might join me one afternoon at the YMCA when Mister Baer is scheduled to address my boxing teams. I am employed by the YMCA, you see, to—"

"Oh I know *that*," he said, and he turned a chair around and straddled it, resting his forearms on the chair's back. He winked at me with his good eye, then reached a hand toward Miss Hémon and, as if he had been with me and Joleen the night we first met Max Baer and he was signaling this fact to me, he caressed Miss Hémon's cheek with the back of his hand. "Ain't Miss Marie-Anne the loveliest woman you ever know—ain't there never been a woman lovelier than her?"

"As the song would have it," Miss Hémon said, and, to my astonishment, she took the hand with which Hawkins was caressing her cheek, and pressed it lightly to her lips. "Hawkins is a terrible flirt, as you can see, Mister Littlejohn, and a most irresistible man."

"Oh yes," Hawkins said. "Like I like to say, 'Ain't no pleasure but pleasure.' So the way I see it is when you ain't got what you want, you take. Ain't that so?"

"It surely is," Miss Hémon said.

"I don't understand," I said.

"That be 'cause you a most jealous man, my friend," Hawkins laughed. "I seen that right away, the look you give me," he added, and saying this, he caressed *my* cheek in the way he had caressed Miss Hemon's. "But you still a brother, and we brothers do get this jealousy thing going time to time. Ain't no crime. But comes the day we can't see what we want, we still be wanting all we can take."

"I have told Hawkins about your diagnosis," Miss Hémon said. "I hope you don't mind."

"No," I said.

"Why else you be here lessen you got a problem with your eyes," Hawkins said. "Ain't nothin' to be ashamed of. Things happen.

Look at me." He closed his good eye, then spoke again: "But I know you, my brother, from once upon a time, and your eyes, they look good still—fact is, all of you do, 'cause you always a fit man like Mister Max. Now Mister Max, he's the best I ever seen. Ain't nobody except maybe the Brown Bomber had the power and the dancing feet both like your man do. And you weren't far behind, what I seen. You had the goods, my brother. So I ask you again—when you gonna let me meet Mister Max and make yourself a righteous man?"

He punched me on the shoulder with his right hand, hard, then wiped off the blow with his left. "I sure can ramble on, tell you that. Ha! Not like you. Your trouble, you ask me, see, you stay at home too much with your woman. You made a good move, coming here. 'Cause this diabetes thing ain't no pleasure. Put my old man in the grave with more pain than you want to know. Went blind first, got a leg cut off, but he was still one mean son of a bitch—pardon my French, Miss Marie-Anne, but hey, you know bad French where you come from too. We both from Lou'siana, did you know that, *mon ami chèr* with the long fingers? So I asking you: Where *you* come from?"

"Texas," I said. "My wife and I are both from Texas, but we have been living in California for many years,"

"Your *wife*?" he said. "I see a ring on that finger, but rings don't always mean we been blessed by the law."

Miss Hémon pushed aside the finger Hawkins was pointing at me. "I think we have completed our introductions for the day, Hawkins," she said.

Hawkins stood. "Ain't no shame, not being married legal," Hawkins said. "Main thing, if you get kids into the world, you raise them with love—and the rest, who cares, ain't that so?"

I stared at him but did not respond.

He poked me in the shoulder with a forefinger. "*Ain't that so?'* " he said again, his voice rising. "*'Ain't that so?'* I asked, so you answer me that, you hear? You ain't such a big shot just 'cause you know Max Baer. You ain't more than a poke to a pig, 'cause look at *me* now. Look at me, and you remember this, like I like to say, Miss Marie-Anne can vouch, 'In the country of the blind, the one-eyed man is king.' Ain't *that* so? You answer me *that. Ain't that so, I asked?*"

Miss Hémon stood and touched the small of Hawkins's back, lightly. "Calm down now, Hawkins," she said. "Calm down now, please. Mister Littlejohn means no offense."

"I mean no offense," I said.

Hawkins bent toward me, and lifted the patch over his right eye so I could see the stitched hollow where an eye had been. "Like I like to say," he said, " 'in the country of the blind the one-eyed man is king,' and you in *my* country now, so you take good care and you be good to this good woman, hear? Or I do mean things like I been known to do."

"You stop this talk at once, Hawkins," Miss Hémon said. "And be gone. Be gone with you."

"I mean no offense neither," he said and, tipping an imaginary hat, he turned and limped from the cafeteria.

"It is often a shock to meet Hawkins for the first time," Miss Hémon said when we were again sitting in her office. "But one gets used to him, and even to have affection for him. Therefore, Mister Littlejohn, I think you may safely let go of your wariness."

"My wariness?"

"Your wariness," she said. "He is a very exuberant man, and his exuberance—his very joy in living, if you will forgive the cliché—is infectious, and more than admirable, don't you agree?"

"When I have let go of my wariness, I will let you know."

"*Touché*, Mister Littlejohn," she said. "Really, though. I have never known anyone quite like him. It is *exciting* to know him, and I find—how best to put it?—that I actually *envy* him at times."

"*Envy* him?" I said.

"Not *him* exactly," she said. "I am, as I hope you'll come to understand, quite content with who *I* am—happy in *my* skin—but it's more his refusal to keep thoughts and feelings hidden, his saying and doing what he wants . . ."

"The only person I have known who has anything like the exuberance you attribute to Hawkins Johnson," I offered, "is Max Baer, a man *I* admit to envying at times. But there are worlds of difference between them."

"Such as?"

"I believe Max Baer's greatest pleasure lies in giving pleasure to others—in conveying to others the joy he feels in living, and in sharing this joy with them."

"And Hawkins?"

"I suspect he acts the way he does because he cannot help himself," I said. "My opinion is, of course, based upon a first impression, but I am not persuaded Mister Hawkins loves life in the way you believe he does. My impression is that he loves himself too much to be capable of doing so."

"My, my," Miss Hémon said. Then, a moment later: "You are smarter than you appear."

"Excuse me?"

"Hawkins Johnson is certainly an indulgent man, and like you, he too is smarter than he appears."

"I do not understand," I said.

"I am teasing you, Mister Littlejohn—playing with you, perhaps?" she said.

"I do not understand," I said again.

"Your manners are impeccable—too much so, I think—yet you do possess a capacity for being direct, and even succinct, when provoked," she said. "And what I find when I provoke you—which I admit to doing—is that you are also an uncommonly intelligent man, and a caring man. In my experience of men, this is a rare combination."

"Thank you."

"May I speak freely?"

"Would I be able to stop you?"

"Correct," she said. "So: what I was thinking of saying is that you do not have much experience of women, do you?"

"I do not understand."

"Exactly," she said, and she raised her left hand in the air to show me her ringless fingers. "Permit me to provide you with some basics. I am not a married woman. I have never been a married woman. I will never be a married woman. A non-conjugal conjugation, yes? My two children are the children of different fathers. They do not and never will know their fathers. I offer you this information so that we will feel free to be the friends we promised to be: to be frank and open with each other, and to hide nothing essential of what we think and feel. So answer me, please, and tell me you understand what I have said."

While she flicked words at me, my head bobbed backwards several times, as if to protect itself from a series of quick, short jabs.

"Tell me," she said again. "Please tell me you understand, Mister Littlejohn."

"But I do not," I said, and was aware, now, of the sound of my heart beating rapidly in the way it would when, at the start of a fight, a referee would be instructing me and my opponent to protect ourselves at all times, and to come out fighting.

"You *choose* not to understand?" she said. "Or you *will* not understand?"

"Perhaps," I said. "Yes. All right then. I choose—*will* choose, however, to reciprocate by stating that Hawkins Johnson seems to have inferred a truth of which I am not embarrassed. Although I wear a wedding band, and although my wife and I, together now for several decades, are legal in the way 'common law' marriages are legal, we have never felt the need to formalize our bond. Although what you say *has* unnerved me, I think I may possibly understand what you have said."

"*Possibly?*" she said.

"Possibly," I said.

"You are also a most attractive man when you ease up on yourself a bit, as you *seem* to be doing," Miss Hémon said. "Therefore: what I can promise is that I will continue to work at making you my good and dear friend, as Doctor Levitzky asked me to."

"Did he really ask that of you?"

"Oh, Mister Littlejohn, you are a wonder," she said. "And you and I are going to have some lovely times together, I expect, and to that end, I have a proposal."

"Please," I said.

"You have seen the lay of the land here—a land where Hawkins Johnson is self-proclaimed king, and a land where I believe you have the potential, perhaps, to rise to the position of crown prince," she said. "I believe you will come to trust me as I trust you, and to enhance *that* possibility—fond word—and because I am, to state the obvious, fond of *you* and wish to cultivate *our* friendship, I propose that you and your wife—Joleen, yes?—come to my home for dinner at the end of the week. You have told me that you lead an insular life, but surely you can shed that insularity for an evening. I would enjoy meeting your wife and I would enjoy having the two of you meet my children. If your son can get away from his studies, perhaps he might join us."

"Thank you," I said. "You are most kind, and . . ."

". . . and quite forward. Hawkins and I are alike in that: when we see or know what we want, we see no reason not to take it. So the answer is yes, yes?"

"I will talk with Joleen."

That Friday evening Joleen and I had dinner at Miss Hémon's home, and we met her children—Anna, who was thirteen, and David, who was eleven. On the following Friday evening Joleen and I made dinner for the three of them in our home, at which dinner Horace Jr. joined us, and on the Friday after that, the three of us again had dinner with Miss Hémon and her children at their home, and thus did we and our families become friends. Joleen and Miss Hémon took to one another as women who are mothers usually do, having in common the many delights and frustrations that accompany the raising of children—"responsibilities without end amen," was the way Miss Hémon put it to Joleen—and her two children were charming, bright, well-mannered, and seemed, at least in our company, not at all self-conscious about their disabilities.

Anna, in the most unobtrusive manner, would lead David from place to place, letting him know where walls, steps, tables, chairs, doors, rooms, and food were located—and David, his hands deftly signing words for Anna, or lightly holding his fingers to her lips— would translate what we were saying that she could not comprehend by lip-reading. Their lack of self-consciousness was epitomized by the pleasure they took in explaining a familiar statue of three monkeys that graced the living room mantel.

"This is our family," Anna would declare in a set piece she delighted in reciting. "David *sees* no evil. I *hear* no evil. And our mother—why she *speaks* no evil . . . except, of course, when she is really *really* angry with one of us."

Horace Jr. told them stories about growing up on the Baer ranch, and of adventures he and Max Jr. enjoyed together, and he recounted stories for them from the Bible in which he noted that many of the principal characters—Isaac, Jacob, Samson, Eli—were blind, and of how Jesus healed the blind, and also of how Homer, the greatest poet of them all, was blind, yet could recite, by heart, his epic poems, *The Iliad* and, Horace Jr.'s favorite, *The Odyssey*, in which tale the wandering Odysseus is made temporarily deaf—his ears stopped up with beeswax so he does not succumb to the seductive songs of the Sirens.

And on the evening he told the story of how Jacob had tricked his blind father so as to steal his father's blessing and inheritance from his brother, Esau, Horace began to invent a story about a blind girl and a deaf boy—brother and sister—who solve crimes by putting together clues unseen and/or unheard by others. He told these stories after dinner, and ended each evening's episode at a moment of peril for the boy and/or the girl, while promising to tell Anna and David what-happened-next when next our families would be together.

It was, of course, a joy for the three of us to see our children delight in one another, and if I had another life, their friendship would doubtless become the matter of a tale more sanguine in its issue than the tale I am setting down here. Perhaps Horace Jr., whose life is spent elaborating on the wonder of stories and storytelling, will one day set down his memories of these evenings when we counted none but happy hours. But, as one of the sages he would quote when taking his leave of us taught, "the day is short, and the work is great . . ." Therefore I will take my leave of our children for a while, and return to the story of what happened after Joleen and

I left the employ of Max Baer, and I came to know Marie-Anne Hémon and Hawkins Johnson.

I began visiting the Lighthouse regularly and, troubling convergence, found that the more often I visited, the more swiftly did my vision decline. The YMCA graciously accommodating to my needs, I signed up for a course in Braille that met on Wednesday afternoons, and would arrive early in order to spend some time with Miss Hémon, and no matter which route I took to or from her office, Hawkins would be lying in wait for me, asking when was I going to introduce him to Max Baer. He would sometimes jab a finger into my shoulder or chest, and because I was determined to not give him the satisfaction of letting him see that he upset me, I would not respond, even when he would back me up against a wall, and pepper me with ramblings that seemed without sense.

"Your trouble, you ask me," he said the one time he irritated me sufficiently to cause me to react, "is that you in love, and being in love like being sick. What they got in common—with being off your nut too—is that there ain't no cure. That's why you gonna wind up one blind lovesick brother, and I gonna be there to tell you who you are and who you ain't."

This was, until the very last time I would see him, the one instance in which I was unable to keep from reacting. I took the hand he was poking me with, and, bending its thumb backwards until I saw pain show itself in his wandering eye, I warned him to leave me be and to get on with his work or I would take measures to see that he was relieved of his duties.

At this point, he pursed his mouth and spit—the spittle gobbed my left eye and cheek—and, slipping away while I wiped at my eye, he told me I was no big shot just because I knew Max Baer, that I was going to be more blind than he would ever be, and that he knew things about me nobody else knew, not even Max Baer, and that if I didn't show him respect—"Oh you better respect me, my brother, or I put your heart in the same grave my father be lying in"—he would show the world what he knew about me and Max, and become a rich man doing so too.

"I gonna be richer than God, you don't treat me right," he said. "And when Miss Marie-Anne, she find out what I know, there go the love of your life too, you be left with nothin,' and I gonna be here to laugh in your face the way I spit in it now."

He sucked in more saliva, but before he could launch another stream of the nasty fluid at me, I cracked him across his eyeless cheek with the back of my hand—a quick, sharp blow that sent him reeling along the corridor wall.

I thought he would come at me with more words and threats, but my act—my showing him the fire that was ever mine when I was aroused—seemed to defeat him, for he merely put a hand to his cheek, mumbled to himself—more whimpering than words—and, picking up his mop and pail, limped away.

I agreed with Miss Hémon's suggestion, endorsed by Doctor Levitzky, that while I still retained relatively normal vision, it would be good for me to visit the Enchanted Hills Camp in order to see for myself the ways people with disabilities learned to accommodate to their deficits. Miss Hémon invited Joleen and Horace Jr. to join us, but they declined, saying they thought it best if I went on my own, and began to construct for myself a community of people, in addition to them, upon whom I could, in the years to come, rely upon for guidance and friendship.

Thus, on the second Saturday morning in June, Miss Hémon and I, along with David and Anna, drove to the camp, located on Mount Veeder, ten miles west of Napa. The weather was balmy, the views along the way lovely, and while we drove we sang songs Anna could not hear, and saw sights David could not see, and in marveling at their skills, I began to learn ways of translating the worlds of silence and darkness into those of seeming sound and light, so that by the time we arrived at the camp I felt exhilarated in much the way I had when I was with Max, following on one of his victories, and I could, though at a remove, revel in *his* untamed expressions of joy.

After we had settled into our separate cabins, and washed up—Miss Hémon and I sharing a cabin with separate rooms and a common bathroom, Anna and David rooming in bunkhouses with boys and girls their own ages, several of whom were not only visually or hearing impaired, but doubly disabled—unable either to see *or* to hear—Miss Hémon took me on a tour of the camp's grounds.

Wherever we wandered we met others: men and women who walked with canes or with guide dogs, or arm in arm with one another; children who, loosely roped together at the waist, were learning to navigate trails on their own; and staff members who were giving lectures (with other staff members translating the lectures into sign language for those who could not hear) to individuals, who, like me, seemed to be first-time visitors to the camp.

When I asked Miss Hémon about attending some of these talks, she informed me that she had taken the liberty of obtaining VIP status for me, and would be my personal guide for the weekend. Did I approve?

"Perhaps," I said.

"*Perhaps?!*" she laughed, and talked about how—her hope—as I lost the ability to see the world, I might also lose some of the naiveté that seemed my devoted accomplice.

"I do not understand," I said.

"Come," she said as she started on a marked trail, green arrows painted on small leather pouches that were nailed to tree trunks every ten or twenty yards. "Please. Come with me, Mister Little-john, and let me show you some of the rather exceptional amenities provided for our amusement and education."

While we walked along the trail, I found myself recalling training camps where Max and I had stayed, and how wonderful it had been for the two of us to be away from the rest of the world, with time to do nothing but eat, sleep, and work out. Enchanted Hills Camp put me in mind, in fact, of Max's favorite training camp, in Lakewood, New Jersey, where he had prepared for his fights against Schmeling, Carnera, Braddock, and Louis, and I laughed, recalling how he would drive Cantwell crazy by his refusal to follow the workout regimens Cantwell had prescribed for him. Max did love the early morning roadwork, however, and enjoyed, at the end of these five- to ten-mile runs, sprinting the last two or three hundred yards and challenging anyone, including his young sparring part-ners, to catch him if they could.

As Miss Hémon and I walked on a path of wood chips that made sweet, crunching sounds beneath our shoes, and then several hun-dred feet along a narrow trail that rose gradually to a lookout point above the lake, during which walk we passed others who were al-ready heading back toward the camp (a bell had rung, signaling the noon hour, which was also the hour for a communal lunch), Miss Hémon talked of the hikes Anna and David would be taking, and of the self-confidence people with deficits of hearing and sight gained from traveling the camp's many trails.

By and by, she said, they would come to forget they lacked one or more of the five senses, because what was more important than senses that might take their leave of us were those that remained. This, she explained, was the gist of a talk she often gave to new members of the Lighthouse—a talk in which she emphasized that if we trained the senses that were still ours, we could learn to take as much pleasure—perhaps more—from the world around us as we could were we blessed with a seemingly "normal" set of five senses.

She led me away from the lookout point and along a footpath that descended into a forest thick with evergreens—pine, fir, red-wood—and large swaths of flowering rhododendron. There had been a sun-shower earlier in the day—the cool spray of rain welcome on a day that was more humid than usual—and the fragrance of pine needles and rhododendron blossoms, intensified by the moisture-laden air, was intoxicating. We walked, without talking, for perhaps ten or twelve minutes, until we came to a small clearing that was home to a gazebo that was in a state of considerable disrepair, some of the crossing limbs that supported a fragile roof looking as if they, along with the roof, could be blown away by the next strong wind. There were two benches in the gazebo, facing one another. I sat on one, and Miss Hémon sat next to me.

"This is where Anna first learned to read lips, which has proven an enormous aid not only to her understanding others," she said, "but also to her ability to speak like a hearing person."

"Oh."

"Would you like me to show you how it is done?"

"Please," I said.

"Then close your eyes and put a finger to my lips, and when I speak—I will mouth words without sound—tell me what you think I have said."

I closed my eyes and put a finger to her lips. Her lips moved.

"'Hello?'" I asked.

"Very good. Now put *two* fingers against my lips."

Her lips were soft, and my head filled with a confusing bouquet of scents and memories. I began to feel strangely light-headed. Without sound, she again talked to my fingers.

"'Mister Littlejohn?'" I asked.

"Ah," she said. "You are an excellent pupil—a fast read, as we say, yes? I am not surprised. I have, from our first moments together, sensed you were a man of great potential whose loss of vision would be of manageable consequence, especially if . . ."

"If what?"

". . . if you would allow yourself to trust me."

"I believe that has happened," I said. "But if . . ."

"Anna and I would practice hour after hour," she said, "and I often think of those hours as having been our happiest times together. As she grew up and had less need for my assistance, however, I sometimes found myself wishing we could return to those early times together."

"I can understand that," I said.

"But you, my friend," she said, "who can hear my voice, and who often shies away from its more aggressive probings—you will never have need of what my daughter has had need, will you?"

"I hope not."

"Still, because it pleases me, will you indulge me a while longer and allow me the pleasure of showing you how she learned to hear *and* to speak?"

"Of course."

"Good," she said. "So now please close your eyes again, and press all *five* of your fingers against my mouth."

What I saw before I did what she asked—the bench across from us, the crossing limbs that held up the gazebo's roof, the trees, flowers, and forest beyond turned suddenly gray and blurred as if the world were veiled behind a low-lying cloud and I was unmoored from earth as from time itself—alarmed me: could my vision experience so precipitous a decline that what I had seen but a few minutes before could suddenly have no recognizable shape or color?

I pressed my eyes closed, and when I did, she mouthed words I hoped—and feared—she would speak, after which, very slowly, she took the tip of my index finger onto her lower lip, and kissed it.

I did not move. Nor did I state the obvious: that although I might eventually lose my vision, there were, as she had said, no indications I was in danger of losing my hearing. Why, then, was it so important that I learn to read lips the way Anna had? Why was it so important that I understand what *their* experience had been like? She bent over and kissed my hand in much the way she had, in her office, kissed Hawkins Johnson's hand—more with her breath than with her mouth—and after that it was her eyes that told me what her lips and tongue had told my fingers, and they asked for a reply.

As if she could infer my answer, she nodded once, and so I kissed her hand in the way she had kissed mine, after which she gestured to me to again close my eyes and to again touch her mouth with my fingers. I did what she asked, and my answer, to the question she asked of my fingers, was that yes, I would very much like to kiss her.

Her lips were warm, and everything that was me—my mouth, heart, hands, skin, and what was left of my mind—was aroused, although the kiss itself was without overt force or passion.

"You have never kissed any woman other than your wife, have you?" she said when we had separated.

"I have not."

"Yet you are remarkably good at it," she said.

"Thank you," I said.

"Still, I wonder: Am I worthy of—am I prepared *for* such a responsibility?"

"Possibly," I said.

"Ah yes," she said. "The land of possibility—far preferable to the land of probability, don't you think?"

"Perhaps."

"But there's also this—can you trust me to continue as your

guide? Will you believe that if you fall—I speak metaphorically, Mister Littlejohn—I will be here to catch you?"

We kissed again, and then again, and when some time later I withdrew my mouth from hers, she touched my cheek with her hand, and spoke: "You are a gentle soul," she said.

"Probably," I said.

She tapped on my lips with her fingertips. "You are a love," she said.

"Possibly," I said, and we both laughed, and I kissed her again—would I ever want to *not* be kissing her?—and her mouth opened to me this time, and I was lost in feelings and sensations of which, in truth, I had had no intimations.

"To repeat," she said when we had again separated. "You *are* a love, Mister Horace Littlejohn. And you *are* a gentle soul, and how surprising it is, given your devotion to a sport that is itself savage in the extreme."

"*Not at all!*" I protested. "Oh not at all! You speak from ignorance, and—"

Her hand firm on the back of my neck, she drew me to her, her eyes demanding my full attention, and she spoke each word as if it were a sentence. "*I – do – not – mean – to – offend,*" she said. "Do you *not* understand me? I intended my words as a compliment to *who – you – are*—to how gentle you are despite having spent so much of your life in battle with others, despite—"

"Not at all," I said again, and found myself drawing upon talks I sometimes gave to the young men I worked with at the YMCA. "Not at all, Miss Hémon, for boxing is a sport—and an art—with an ancient and honorable history that has, with reason, been known as the 'sweet science.' Although its participants may suffer injury, such injury usually results from ignorance in the same manner that those who are injured in other athletic contests, or in automobile or airplane accidents are injured—because they are not well-trained, or take liberties that are unwise, or—"

"Or what?" she said. "How can you compare driving an automobile with attacking someone so as to render that person unconscious? How can you believe that if . . . ?"

"Please," I said. "Consider this: Do men who fight according to rules that encourage them to protect themselves at all times, and with hands swathed in tape and leather—do they die with greater frequency at their vocation than men who work in coal mines, or who build bridges and tunnels? Do they die with greater frequency than men who choose to defend our nation, or patrol our cities' streets, or plunge into burning buildings? Do they die with greater frequency than men who go out to sea in fishing boats, or—"

She stopped my mouth with a kiss so fierce—her fingernails digging into the skin of my neck and shoulders, her teeth tearing at my lips and tongue—that even while lost in a desire to respond to her with a ferocity—and a rage—of my own, I found myself wondering how, when she and I returned to the camp, we would explain wounds I feared would be visible to others . . . and I then wondered what she might think were I to reveal this thought to her—were she to learn that in a moment of near feral abandon—a moment when I was tasting the salty sweetness of blood and could not know if it were hers, mine, or ours—I remained a slave to thoughts that seemed terribly rational.

"In addition to which," I stated when we were again sitting side by side, "it is a way of defending ourselves from those who would do us harm. Thus, at the YMCA, my young men will have the benefit for the rest of their lives of knowing how to protect themselves and those they love, and they will also know the pleasure one knows, as in any athletic enterprise, or in any of the arts, for that matter— in music, or painting, or dance—when we work in a diligent and disciplined way to perfect a craft."

"My goodness," Miss Hémon said. "Given the fervor with which you put forth your views, and given, too, what I know of your son's love of the Bible, and what you have told me of the Bible's importance to you and Joleen—I must wonder: Have you ever considered the ministry? For you clearly have a gift—a zeal—for preaching that, if devoted exclusively to the world of boxing, might go unrealized for more worthy matters, especially if—"

"Do not belittle me," I said, and I stood and walked away.

At the edge of the clearing, I turned and glared at her. She took in a long breath, after which she gestured to me to return to her.

"Please," she said. "Please, Horace . . ."

It was the first time she had not called me "Mister Littlejohn," and noticing—this too was a surprise—that her eyes were moist with tears, I returned, and stood in front of her.

"It is not my habit to humble myself before others," she said. "I admire the passion you have for what you do, and I am embarrassed by my ignorance of matters of which you speak, as well as by ways I have misjudged you. So: Will you forgive me?"

When she reached toward me, I took her hand in mine, and when she touched the space on the bench next to her, I sat. A minute or so later, she spoke: "May I return, then, to what I was saying about you before . . . before I rudely . . ."

"If it pleases you to do so."

"It does—oh it does," she said, "for you *are* a love and a truly gentle soul, and so I am wondering what we shall do to fulfill the needs and desires of your love and of your soul, which needs and desires, I assure you, have their counterparts in who *I* am and who *I* wish to be."

We sat side by side for a while without talking, and I was relieved to find that, though the scene in front of me remained clouded, it had begun to regain its recognizable shapes and colors.

6   Brothers

O that thou wert as my brother, that sucked the breasts of my mother! When I should find thee without, I would kiss thee; yea, I should not be despised. (8:1)

On a Tuesday afternoon, the last week of June 1958, while I was having lunch in the staff lounge of the YMCA, Miss Patricia Fontaine, a secretary in our office, entered the room, as she usually did at this hour, and distributed the day's mail. In addition to correspondence having to do with our teams—schedules for upcoming tournaments, equipment we had ordered—there was a small, square envelope of a kind that often contained a greeting card or an announcement. I opened it, and read:

Monday 23 June 1958

Dear Horace . . . and becoming dearer . . .

Is it—perhaps? probably? possibly?—an entire day since we were together? Impossible! It seems like years and, at the same time, but a few minutes ago. I miss you. And yet I am comforted by the thought that . . .

Miss Hémon went on to write in ways as elegant as they were candid about new responsibilities she had chosen to bear, and about pleasures she hoped we would continue to enjoy until they became so sublime as to seem almost (but not quite) *un*-bearable. To this end, she was most cordially inviting me to visit her in her home for several hours on Wednesday, June 25, at half past noon, at a time when I might otherwise be engaged in tutoring my young charges or studying Braille at the Lighthouse, and when she might otherwise be teaching a class or pushing papers from one side of her desk to the other, so that, with the very same hands we would otherwise have been using for such tasks, we might be kind to one another in ways yet to be determined.

And so began the happiest days and hours of my life, their pleasures doubtless enhanced by the fact that we were, Miss Hémon and I, obliged out of consideration for others to hide the fact of the unexpected course our friendship had taken. "Stolen waters are sweet, and bread eaten in secret most pleasant," Proverbs tells us. True enough, although I do not believe our love was sweeter *because* it was secret, for were this so, my love for Max and Joleen—loves that compelled concealment—would have remained the supreme and transcendent loves of my life. And despite my romantic proclivities,

I would sometimes admit to Miss Hémon that she and I were probably not all that different from others—that our situation was comprised of the kinds of ordinary complications and secrecies—the obstacles *to* love—that accompanied what many individuals in love experienced.

The obstacles to our being able to be together whenever we wished and in whatever way we wished were clear enough, of course—my devotion to Joleen, Miss Hémon's devotion to her children, and our desire not to impose upon them complications and confusions that would arise from knowledge of who she and I had become to one another. Unlike the love she had for Anna and David, and the love I had for Joleen, Max, and Horace Jr., however—loves that would pass from this world only when we passed from this world—our expectations, from the beginning, were realistic, for we seemed, separately, to have come to the same conclusion: that free as we were in our love *for* one another, yet was our love destined to be ever a moment away from perishing as swiftly as it had come into being. We were free in our love, that is, because we loved without either expectations *or* hope—because we were acutely aware that, as Virgil wrote, in a line Horace Jr. loved to quote, "*Optima dies . . . prima fugit,*" which he translated as "The best days are the first to flee."

Miss Hémon and I met whenever and wherever we could—in her home and mine (when Joleen and our children were away); on walks in parts of San Francisco where we felt reasonably certain we would meet no one we knew (or who, if they knew us, would not *see* us); on weekends at Enchanted Hills Camp; for wild and quick assignations in her office (the door locked); and, like randy adolescents whose lustful longings put the fulfillment of desire above patent dangers, in unlikely settings I will not here name. Nor will I particularize the pleasures we knew, or their astonishing variations, or recount with any further specificity when, where, how often, or for what lengths of time we met. I do not shy away from telling of such matters because to do so would demean or diminish our love, but because I wish, simply, to let what was ours remain ours. I will, however, note this: that I never loved Miss Hémon more than when I watched her tending to her children. This, in addition to her beauty, her sensuality, her wit, her intelligence, and her kindness, was for me ever the great aphrodisiac.

There was this too: that I felt she would protect me with the same fierce determination with which she would her own children. Being with her and her children put me in mind—curious realization—of Max's desire to protect me. In particular, I found myself recalling a time in Chicago, on a scorching August evening in 1932, the temperature and humidity approaching one hundred degrees, when I was accompanying him on his rounds of several jazz clubs he liked to visit. The following evening he would fight a second time against Ernie Schaaf, a man who had defeated him badly during their first match two years earlier in New York City's Madison Square Garden. It was in this second fight, in Chicago, that he would knock Schaaf unconscious. Several months later, when Schaaf died after a bout with Carnera, it would be Max, and the savage beating he had rendered Schaaf, and not Carnera, who would be seen as the cause of Schaaf's death.

But on the night before he rendered Schaaf unconscious, Max did not know this would happen, and he was enjoying, among other things, the pleasure it gave him to know that Cantwell was back in our hotel, having one of his famous fits because Max was, yet again, out on the town and breaking all training rules.

Max had as his other companion that evening a young, beautiful jazz singer named Leslie Pearl, and the three of us were standing at the bar while a jazz trio was on break, Max holding forth with one of his tall tales, when a man approached him, tapped him on the shoulder, and asked if he had read the sign.

"I'm not into astronomy," Max laughed, "but they tell me I'm an Aquarius, which means I got a serious and sunny nature. How about you?"

The man, shorter than Max by three or four inches but weighing a good twenty or thirty pounds more, pointed to a sign above the bar that read "We Serve Whites Only."

"So you're okay then," Max said. "They can serve you here."

"But not this nigra next to you," the man said.

The room became suddenly quiet. Max smiled broadly, put an arm around Leslie.

"Get lost, Mister, okay?" Max said, and he put his other arm around me. "We're here to have a good time and we don't want some Sad Sack Sam messing up our party, okay? And this man here, he's my right-hand man, see—my *best* friend."

"And who the hell are *you*?" the man said.

"Why I'm *his* friend!" Max said.

I saw the bartender take a baseball bat out from under the counter, slap the heft of it against his palm several times.

"Look," Max said to the man. "Like the blind man said when he pissed into the wind, 'It's all coming back to me now!' Get it?"

"Get out," the man said, and he took the baseball bat from the bartender. "We don't like nigras much around here, but we hate nigra *lovers* even worse."

"Too bad for you," Max said, "because, like I said, you're pissing into the wind, Mister, and if you don't want to wind up blind in both eyes, which operation I'd be pleased to perform free of charge, I suggest you put that toothpick down and vamoose. 'Cause if you're blind, see—in your eyes, not in what passes for the slop you got between your ears—in a minute or two you won't be able to *see* that sign—or my friend either."

Someone whispered in the man's ear.

The man took a step back. "You're *Max Baer*?"

"That's what they tell me, and let me tell you that I don't mind being him one bit," Max said, and he took the bat out of the man's hand, and tossed it to the bartender, to whom he now spoke. "Hey— I'd get rid of that sign, if I were you, okay? It's making your customers uncomfortable."

The bartender froze where he was.

"*Now!*" Max commanded.

The bartender did what Max asked. The man who had confronted Max backed away, told Max he didn't mess with killers or kikes, and hurried out the door.

"Ladies and gentlemen," Max announced, holding up my right hand and Leslie's left. "A TKO, two minutes of the first round! And to celebrate the victory, drinks are on the house—right, bartender?—so everybody drink up and don't forget to have a good time!"

On the fourth Friday after we had returned from our first visit to the Enchanted Hills Camp, I arrived at Miss Hémon's home an hour or so earlier than usual. My Golden and Silver Gloves teams had a competition in Northridge the next morning, and I had cut our training session short, and urged my young men to have an early dinner and a long night's sleep. My hope was that Anna and David might be off playing, and that Miss Hémon and I might enjoy some private time before Joleen and Horace Jr. arrived. But as I was turning the corner on Alabama Street, I saw a man walking across her backyard, then leaving the yard through a loose slat in the fence that enclosed the yard. The shuffling walk and bandana were familiar, and I told myself that my eyesight was not as reliable as it had once been, and that Hawkins Johnson was hardly the only man of color in San Francisco who wore a bandana or walked with a limp.

Before I could reflect on what I had seen, though, I became aware of cries coming from Miss Hémon's home. I hurried up her steps and, without knocking, entered. Miss Hémon and Anna were in the living room, Miss Hémon straitjacketing Anna from behind the way I might have held a fighter determined to attack his opponent after a bout was over. Anna was thrashing about wildly while David stood a few feet away, staring at his mother and sister as if he could actually see them.

Miss Hémon was talking softly into her daughter's ear. "I love you, sweetheart, and everything will be all right," she was saying. "I love you and I love you, and everything will be all right, so just let me hold you a while longer. Don't fight me, sweetheart. Please. I love you, and everything will be all right. You'll see. I love you and everything will be all right . . ."

The only time I had ever seen a child in such a frenzied agony had been when I was younger than David was now, and my father had had my older brother Simon tie Joleen to a chair so he could whip her across her chest and legs with a willow switch, and while this memory blazed through my mind, and while I listened to Miss Hémon's voice as if I, too, like David, might draw consolation from it, it did not occur to me that Anna could not hear the words her mother was speaking.

Why then was Miss Hémon whispering to her . . . ? And why was she gazing at me with such a fierce expression? She seemed not at all startled to see me there, while for my part I felt disoriented— like a child about to do what as a child I did not dare do—to stride forward and snatch the willow switch from my father's hand while crying out that he was never ever again to touch or come near to my sister!

"Get out, Mister Littlejohn," Miss Hémon said. "Get out at

once. This is not your business. This is not your family. Leave us be. Please."

I kneeled in front of Anna, who continued to wail away, her thin body heaving in and out. I set two fingers against her mouth—ready to pull them back if she moved to bite—and tapped upon her upper lip.

"Listen to your mother," I said. "She loves you as I do, and everything *is* going to be all right. Can you understand?"

At my words, her screaming abated slightly, and I wiped at her eyes with the sleeve of my shirt.

"I'm sorry," she said a minute later.

Miss Hémon was now attending to David, and it was only when she did that I became aware of a large lump on his forehead.

I went into the kitchen, wrapped ice in a dishcloth, returned, and placed the ice pack against David's forehead, telling him to hold it there for as long as he could bear doing so.

Miss Hémon and Anna sat on the couch, Anna's head resting against her mother's shoulder. "I'm sorry, Mama," Anna said. "But it hurt *so* much. You don't know. You *can't* know what it's like . . ."

"That's true," Miss Hémon said.

"I get scared," Anna said. "That's all. I just get scared. It hurts so much that I get scared."

"We all get scared sometimes," Miss Hémon said. "I'll wager that even Mister Littlejohn gets scared sometimes."

"I do," I said. "I surely do."

"What seems to happen at times—" Miss Hémon explained when Anna and David had gone off on their own, and I watched her prepare dinner "—what Anna tells me happens—is that a series of small explosions take place inside her head. They arrive without warning, become louder and louder, and she becomes frightened they have no way out and are going to blow her head wide open—that her brains will scatter everywhere, and that she will disappear."

I expressed my sympathy, and my admiration for the way she had been with Anna, then asked about the man I had seen leaving through her backyard, and told her he reminded me of Hawkins Johnson.

"That *was* Hawkins," she said. "He often comes by to help me with chores, and with the children."

"Did *he* do anything to cause Anna's fright?" I asked.

"Of course not."

"And the lump on David's head?"

"David ran into a wall—in the upstairs hallway," she said. "When he is very upset he does that—he will turn in circles to make himself dizzy, then charge ahead until something stops him."

"But how can you . . . ?"

"It is my life, Mister Littlejohn," she said. "Do you have any other questions?"

"Do you feel safe when Hawkins is here?"

"*Safe?!*" Miss Hémon said. "What kind of question is that? Like you, Hawkins is a dear friend." She bent toward me as if to confide a secret. "I certainly feel safer with him than I do with you, given the things *you* have tried to do with me."

"But I thought you enjoyed—"

She stopped my words with a quick kiss. "Oh Horace, you are a wonder," she said, "Taking advantage of your innocence has become one of my great pleasures." Then: "Hawkins thought you might arrive early today," she said. "That was why he left when he did, and—"

"But how would he know, unless . . . ?"

"—and he had come here to tell me that your friend Max Baer will be visiting the YMCA next week."

"And so—"

"And so he was hoping I might put in a word with you on his behalf so that he might meet the man."

"I don't think that will be possible."

"It would mean a lot to him."

"Hawkins has said things to me that suggest he would use the occasion to malign Max's character," I said.

"I would think Mister Baer is capable of defending himself," she said.

"I see no reason to arrange a situation in which Hawkins would confront Max in a way that would be disruptive," I said. "But now that he has chosen to come to you—to involve you—I will talk with him, and after that—"

"You will tell all, yes?"

"Yes."

She took my hands in hers. "We should have no secrets from one another," she said. "We should not hold back ever, not even for fear of hurting the other. We have agreed to that—agreed that it is at the heart of what we have found in and with one another. So rare, Horace. So rare, don't you agree?"

"Yes," I said.

She let go of my hands. "Oh, we can dissemble a bit about things that are without consequence—" she said "—if I like your haircut, if you like my new dress—and we don't have to say *everything* that comes to mind simply because, well, it comes to mind. Privacy yes, secrecy no, is the way I see it. Our thoughts and musings—our fantasies—they can remain ours, don't you agree?"

"I will talk with Hawkins at the next opportunity," I said. "But for now I prefer to talk about Anna and David's mother. I have never known a mother as loving and calm—as *patient*—as you."

"And strong," she said, smiling. "You forgot 'strong.' I am very strong. Care to feel my biceps?"

I felt her biceps. "Impressive," I said.

"May I feel yours?" she asked, and then, of a sudden, as if feeling the weight of what had happened with Anna and David for the first time, her body sagged and, eyes closed, she leaned against the kitchen sink to keep from collapsing.

"Are you all right?" I asked, and rested my hands on her back.

"No," she said. "But I will be. What I worry about, you see, is what they will do—how they will cope—should anything happen to me. I worry and I wonder, Mister Littlejohn, because they have no father, no family—no aunts, uncles, grandparents. What, then, will they *do* if something happens to me? Do you have the answer to *that*? Tell me, please. What will they *do*? Who will care for them? Who will know *how* to care for them?"

"But nothing will happen to you," I said. "And should something happen, I . . ."

She waved away my words, stood up tall, and returned to the stove. "Sometimes I think I shouldn't love them as much as I do— that it's truly wanton of me," she said. "*Wanton*, Mister Littlejohn. Wanton and irresponsible and . . ."

"And what?" I asked.

"I'm glad you asked," she said, "for in addition to being wanton and irresponsible, I am also melancholy at times. I am not always the cheerful mother, devoted employee, and magnificent lover of whom you are so inordinately fond. I thought you should know that. And sometimes I despair of a life in which I will be forever tending to Anna and David, never knowing with any certainty that they will be all right, or that there will ever be a life for me— or for them—beyond love and worry. Because as I've said before, it's all love and worry, don't you see? And why is that, do you suppose?"

"I am certain you will tell me," I said.

"Of course," she said, and she pulled me to her, took my left ear between her teeth, bit down hard. "Because," she whispered, "when it comes to our children, there is no safety."

"There is no safety," I repeated.

"There is no safety," she said. "I figured that out a long time ago, and once I did, I concluded that, if there is no safety, then the only thing worth having—worth *taking*—is pleasure. Do you understand *that*?"

"Perhaps," I said.

"But since, with the children here, you cannot give me the pleasure I would most like to have—the pleasure that makes all else disappear—I will ask you to do something else for me. Do you have your kit with you?"

"My kit?"

"For the diabetes."

"Of course," I said. "I keep it with me always. Doctor Levitzky said—"

"Then let us give thanks to Doctor Levitzky," she said, "and please go fetch your kit, and we will adjourn for a few minutes to the basement where I will take pleasure from watching you inject yourself. And after that, while I occupy myself with final preparations for dinner, I hope you will do me the additional favor of going upstairs and checking in on the children to make sure they are all right."

I looked into David's room first, but the children were not there. Then I looked into Anna's room and I was so taken aback by what I saw—David standing on a footstool, eyes closed, hands at his sides, kissing Anna, who wore a blindfold over her eyes—that I nearly cried out. I could hear my heart pound inside my ears, and I backed away quickly so that they would not know I had seen them, and so that I could collect my thoughts.

I also reproached myself, for I recalled that on the very first evening we had had dinner here, and I had seen how affectionate Anna and David were with one another, I had thought of how Joleen and I had been with one another as children, and I had wondered for an instant—foul thought of which I immediately chastised myself—whether they too might some day be to each other as Joleen and I had been.

I tiptoed downstairs, where Miss Hémon, in the kitchen, wiped her hands on her apron, put her arms around my neck and gave me a long, lingering kiss.

"That's for being so kind to my children," she said. "It's the quick way to this woman's heart."

"I see that," I said.

Then: "Is everything all right?" she asked, her brow furrowed. "The children?"

I realized that Miss Hémon did not know, nor could she have any reason to suspect the true relationship between me and Joleen, and could not therefore suspect why seeing what I had seen had alarmed me. At the same time, I imagined telling Max what I had seen—telling him *why* seeing this brother and sister kissing had so upset me. "Holy mackerel," I could hear him say. "I've seen and done lots of crazy stuff in my time, Horace, but to do it with your own sister—hey, that's really sick, you ask me."

"They were kissing," I said to Miss Hémon. "But not passionately. It was as if they were trying something out—experimenting perhaps. David was standing on a footstool, and they were not embracing."

Miss Hémon laughed.

"Pecking," I went on. "They seemed to be pecking at each other."

"And you were worried, weren't you, that they were performing some dark, secret act—"

"Well . . ." I began. "Not worried perhaps, but . . ."

"Anna has a birthday party tomorrow night, girls and boys, and she told me her girlfriend Diane said there would be kissing games at the party," Miss Hémon said.

"Oh yes," I said. "I recall when Horace Jr. attended his first kissing games party. Yes."

"They're practicing," Miss Hémon said. "That's all. How sweet."

"How sweet," I repeated.

"Yet you *were* worried, weren't you?"

"A bit," I said. "Not very, but . . ."

"You are the dearest man I have ever known," she said. "And the most innocent. How did I get to be so lucky?"

"Practice?" I asked, and when I did, she slugged me hard, on the arm.

"You can be mean too, can't you?" she said.

"Perhaps."

"I like that. Hmmm. Perhaps we can take our cue from my children," she said. "I had no brothers *or* sisters, so incest was a possibility that was never available to me. But you, Horace?"

"I had three sisters," I said. "But I left them, and home, when I was fifteen years old."

"Perhaps we can pretend," she said. "You can be the brother and I can be your sister, and one day when we come home from school early . . ."

She kissed me again, held to me. "What's so wonderful," she said softly, "is the sense that, with you, I'm starting all over again— that with you I can do and say anything I want, without fear and without doubt and without all the other vexations that have plagued me across a lifetime. And I sense—I *know*—you're feeling the same way."

"Yes," I said, and would have embraced her more tightly, but I heard footsteps—Anna and David, coming down the stairs—and so we separated, and I picked up plates and silverware, and went into the dining area to set the table for dinner.

When I arrived at the Lighthouse the following Wednesday afternoon for my Braille class, instead of going directly to Miss Hémon's office, as had become my habit, I went to the library so that I could work for a half hour or so on the Braille assignments our instructor had given us the previous week. When I entered, neither Miss Duncan nor her two assistants were there.

I sat at a desk, opened a box of cards, closed my eyes, and began reading the words on the cards with my fingers, skipping over those of which I was unsure, and setting them aside so I could return to them later. After several minutes, Miss Duncan appeared. Her hair tumbling down past her shoulders, she was in the process of pinning it back up.

"Well, Mister Littlejohn, we have arrived early today, haven't we?" she said. "What a pleasant surprise."

She smoothed down the wrinkles in her dress, and withdrew several pins from her mouth—how she had spoken with them *in* her mouth was unclear to me—and asked if I had visited with Miss Hémon yet.

"I have been working on my Braille cards," I said.

At this point, Hawkins emerged from the back room, Miss Duncan's two assistants, Pamela and Gail, with him.

He grinned, and spoke without embarrassment: "So now you be seeing again how what I say about the country of the blind be true," he said. "And ain't that what you come here to see, my brother?"

"Do not call me brother," I said.

"Ah, but I *am* your brother," he said. "I be your brother in pleasure, my friend. Like the Good Book says, the more sadness the more joy, the more pain the more pleasure, and you and me been taking our share of pleasure with the ladies, wouldn't you say?"

"Hawkins!" Miss Duncan scolded. "Please. You stop at once. What will Mister Littlejohn think if you talk like this?"

"He'll think I be a man lucky as him," he said. "Way I figure, he got the upstairs covered, where Miss Hémon be, and I got the main floor covered, and that way *everybody* gets to be happy, and that's what God wants for us, ain't it, that we be his happy children down here?"

"As to Miss Hémon," I said. "You will not refer to her in a disrespectful way, or . . ."

"Or what?" he answered. "You gonna punch out my lights so I get to call the cops on you? Got witnesses right here—*très* beautiful witnesses too, don't you think? Or you gonna get your boy Max Baer to help you, 'cause when it comes to the ladies, I hear he's the man they love even more than they love you and me."

"Do not mind Hawkins," Miss Duncan said, picking up a telephone receiver. "Appearances can be deceiving, and I trust you will not draw false conclusions. Would you like me to let Miss Hémon know you are here?"

"No thank you," I said. I looked at Pamela and Gail, who stood side by side in matching white blouses and gray cardigan sweaters. "Are you all right?" I said to them.

They responded to my question by giggling, hands over their mouths as if they were Ziegfeld girls in an old silent movie, and I closed my eyes, then opened them again to make sure I was not dreaming.

"We are a particularly close-knit family here at the Lighthouse," Miss Duncan said, fingering the necklaces that rested on her bosom. "Do you see what I mean, Mister Littlejohn?"

"And Miss Hémon," Hawkins said, "she say you be ready to talk with me, so let's go do it."

He took me by the arm, tried to turn me toward the door. I pushed him away, but he shadowed me out of the room and along the hallway.

"Like they like to say, no time like the present," he said. "I seen you in the ring, know you a man don't scare easy, so why you be scared of old Hawkins who just wants to be your friend the way he be to the ladies, and when I say ladies I don't just mean the ladies here."

"What *do* you mean?"

"I mean your wife—Joleen her name now, right?—I be talking about her too."

I grabbed him by the front of his shirt. "What are you talking about?" I said.

"I talking about how your wife—so-*called* wife, because she ain't legal, I hear—and how she's one smart lady, and not just some dumb—"

"Has Miss Hémon talked with you about my marriage?"

"Didn't have to," he said. "'Cause the way I see it, women get what they want same as us, and your wife, we gonna call her that, out of respect—so how about we get to what we here for? How about telling me how I gonna meet Mister Max Baer, show him what I got."

"Which is—?"

"All right then," he said. "Since you wanting me to spell it out, I do you the favor." He looked to both sides of the hallway. Then: "What I got to show, see, is pictures of you and him, that's what I got, and you can tear out my tongue or poke out my good eye, but those pictures still be here to do their work."

"But *how*—?" I began.

"You be patient, you learn it all," he said, "'cause what's happening here is I only asking you to let me *talk* with the man, tell him what I been saving up so he can give me what I want."

"Which is?"

"The money, man," he said. "What else? The money. Because I'm a simple man, see, and I want the money that gonna set me free so I don't be cleaning out toilets and mopping floors and sneaking around for my pleasures the rest of my life. And let me tell you, when it comes to taking pleasures, Hawkins Johnson is your man. You don't believe that, you one sorry old black man lets his sister lead him around by the you-know-what."

That was when I slammed my fist into his gut. He doubled over, sucked air.

"You watch your mouth," I said, "or it will lose what teeth it has left, do you hear me?"

He inhaled huge gobs of air. "You touch me again, and you be one dead man," he said when he had recovered. "You wouldn't be the first, you know. And what I got to show, it show you I mean business, 'cause it gonna show you how I been following you *years* now, see—years and years, all the way from Lou'siana and Texas—kept me *alive*, oh yes it did, keeping my eye on you and her, so I got to thank you for that."

He started to slip down along the wall, so I pulled him up by his shirt, kept him upright.

"*You'll* be the dead man," I said. "And when you're gone, who will miss you, Hawkins? Who will care?"

He tried to spit at me, but I grabbed him by the throat so that he could do nothing but gurgle helplessly. "I am known as a peaceful man," I said, "but I *can* be roused. Be assured of that."

When I let go of his throat, he spit tobacco juice on the floor, then leaned close, spoke in a low voice. "I know who you are, see, and who your wife is, and what Mister Max Baer done with you both," he said. "Oh yeah, it be the death of him and his family, his good name too, news gets out and around—so you do all you want to me with them long-fingered bones, but it's time. It's time, see? It's time to go and show the man what we got."

I struck at him again—quick left-right-left blasts to the body—and then, as he fell toward me, a rabbit punch to the base of his skull, a chop hard enough to put him out cold but not enough to kill. Crazed as I felt—*my* head ready to explode—yet was I level-headed enough not to do anything that would leave marks. I watched him slide down the wall, collapse onto the floor. Without going upstairs to see Miss Hémon, I left the building, took a streetcar to the YMCA, and while my boys continued their exercises and sparring, I put on my leather glove wraps and worked the speed bag at the highest rate I could without losing control, and my boys' delight in having me there when they had not expected me, and the admiration in their eyes for the skills I displayed, gave my heart ease.

Max arrived at the YMCA on Monday afternoon, August 24, 1959, accompanied by a young actress, Ilana Roza Bator, who had long flaming red hair, and wore a backless green silk dress. We had set up a boxing ring in the main gymnasium, and Max glad-handed the people assembled there—my boxers, the director of the YMCA, our staff, board members, and major donors and sponsors—and he introduced us all to Ilana, told us she was from Budapest, had arrived in Hollywood three months before, would be starring in a Warner Brothers spectacle about David and Bathsheba, and that while she prepared for the part, he was helping her learn how to cope with producers, directors, and assorted other West Coast predators. Fishermen too, he added, to laughter, which was why he was showing her San Francisco.

He had also brought his accompanist, Leo Bukzin, with him—Leo often worked with Max and Maxie Rosenbloom on their tours—for whom we had brought in an upright piano, and Max announced that before we got to footwork in the ring, he and Ilana had a surprise for us. Leo played a rippling intro, and then Max and Ilana broke into a soft-shoe to "Tea for Two," and when they were done, Max told the young boxers to get in line behind him and Ilana.

"It ain't that hard—if a lummox like me can do it, so can you, and here's the way it goes," he said, and he started in teaching my boxers the basics—the brush, flap, shuffle, and ball change—and as soon as they caught on, he showed them the time-step, and the "Jackson Heights crossover," and told them they'd soon be dancing rings around their mystified opponents. Then he asked everyone to join in singing, and pretty soon it was as if we were on a sound stage at Warner Brothers, the air filled with music, and my boxers dancing in a chorus line, after which Max had me pass around jump ropes, and he and the boxers—I joined them—began skipping rope in time to the music.

"Hey listen," he said when we took a break and stepped away from the others. "I went to the doctor this morning before I picked up Ilana, and he told me he had good news and bad news. 'So give me the bad news first,' I said. 'Well, Max, the bad news is that you have a serious heart problem,' he said, 'and unless you change your ways and take better care of yourself, you may not make it to the end of the year.' So I said, 'Well, thanks for shooting straight with me, Doc, but what's the good news?' 'The *good* news?' the doc said. 'Oh the good news is that before you came here this morning, I screwed my nurse.'"

Max burst out laughing, pounded me on the back, and gestured to Leo to cut the music. Then Max got the crowd clapping, a slow one-two beat, accent on the second beat—one-*two*, one-*two*—and when the beat had gone on for a while, and Leo had started playing a tinkly burlesque number, Max stripped to the waist, revealing his gorgeous chest and shoulders—my boxers cheered and whistled—and he tore off his trousers, hopped through the ropes and into the ring, and asked who was going be the first guy to get in there and knock him all the way to Alcatraz.

"I may be old," he said, "but I'm as strong as I ever was!" He glanced down toward his waist. "Why now I can bend it!"

My boxers laughed, many of the women covered their eyes, and when Max beckoned to me, I entered the ring, stripped down to my trunks, which, in preparation, I had worn beneath my street clothes. The cheering grew louder. Two of my fighters now entered the ring, wrapped our hands in tape, put on our gloves, and laced them up for us.

I put on my padded headgear, but when one of the boys offered headgear to Max, he said no thanks, that he didn't have any brains left for anyone to knock out. He pointed to the Star of David on the left leg of his trunks, and asked if it was kosher to wear it at a Young Men's *Christian* Association, or maybe I had a cross of Jesus he could pin on the other leg, and then he announced that what people should be on the lookout for were not stars or crosses, or the punches we threw, but the way we bobbed and weaved to keep punches away so our mothers would still love our gorgeous mugs, and that though he was a pretty fair defensive boxer, they were about to see a guy—me—who was the best of the best.

The bell rang, and we danced around one another, and Max faked a left to the stomach, came over quickly with a right cross, and I brushed it away.

"See what I mean!" he cried out. "See what style this man has! Good manners too, 'cause that was a wicked right *cross* I just threw, and he flicked it away like he was telling me to forget the funny business or I'd be seeing *stars*, right?"

We traded punches, Max skipping away every fifteen or twenty seconds to joke with the crowd—patter I was familiar with—and when the bell rang ending the round, instead of going to his corner, he went to the center of the ring, and held up a hand to stop the applause.

"Oh you ain't seen nuthin' yet," he said. "'cause Horace and I got a few more tricks in our bag, but first I got things to say that are serious, and I know that's hard to believe, all the clowning I do, but I really got some serious things to say today. Okay? Are you with me?"

The crowd shouted its approval, and Max gestured to them to gather in closer to the ring.

"Any of you know what tomorrow is—what anniversary we got coming up?" he asked.

Nobody did.

"Well, I'll tell you then," Max said. "Tomorrow's gonna make twenty-nine years since I knocked out a fine young fighter in this town name of Frankie Campbell," he said. "Now I know you know about him because you boys on Horace's Golden Gloves teams got scholarships with his name on it. Frankie was a good man, see, and one helluva fighter, and he died because . . . because . . ."

Max swallowed hard. I moved towards him but he waved me away.

". . . because I hit Frankie Campbell with the last blow he ever felt in this world, and it did something funny to his brain, and we lost him the next day," Max said. "And now I'm gonna introduce you to a man who wasn't with us when it happened on that day, but, like me, he's a man who thinks about Frankie Campbell every day of his life. Ladies and gentlemen, let's have a warm welcome for Frankie Campbell Jr.!"

A stocky, well-built young man, standing at the rear of the crowd, waved to us.

"Come on up and say a few words to us, will you?" Max asked, but Frankie Campbell Jr. shook his head sideways, took a step backwards, waved again. "He's good looking and shy like his dad was, and we can understand why he wouldn't want to come up here on a day like this," Max went on. "It would be hard for the best of us, me included, if it was my old man we were talking about. Now Frankie Jr. was just a few months old when his father left this world, and do you know what?" Max pointed to the ceiling. "I bet your father's up there looking down on us and being real proud of you, Frankie, and of how you went and got a college degree at Notre Dame, and how you got your own family and kids now. And you know what else I bet he's thinking up there? He's thinking that if he had it to do over again, he'd step into that ring and give it his best, and do you know why? Do you? *Do* you?"

The gymnasium was silent.

"Well I'll tell you why," Max said. "Because he loved the sport the way I love the sport, and Horace loves the sport, and all of you young men on Horace's teams love the sport, that's why. Because if you don't find something in your life you love—really love—life ain't worth a plugged nickel. Because hey—look at me and what boxing gave me, okay? Because it gave me things I never would of had if not for this great sport. It gave me friends, and a wife and kids, and money, and a chance to make people happy, and—" he glanced at Ilana "—and it gave me a few other benefits too, right?"

Ilana waved to the crowd.

"And it gave Frankie Campbell the way to marry a woman *he*

loved," Max went on, "and to provide for her, and bring little Frankie Jr. into the world so he could be here today to honor his father's memory. So when me and Horace, who was with me that day and held Frankie's head in his own hands—when Horace and I put on a little show, and then some of you boys go at it, we're gonna know that Frankie Campbell is looking down and smiling to see us doing the one thing that makes everything else okay, ain't that right, Frankie?"

Max turned his eyes upwards, and we all did the same, and I almost expected, for a moment, consummate showman that Max was, that we were going to see Frankie Campbell floating up there, and hear his voice pour down blessings on us. Max pulled me to him, an arm around my shoulder, and as had ever been the case, I could not tell if he was being sincere, or playing at being sincere, or if he knew the difference. He talked to me through the opening in my head gear: "So I said to the doc, 'I also get this ringing in my ears all the time, so what should I do about it?' and the doc said, 'Don't answer it, Max.'"

Then, to the crowd. "And in honor of Frankie, and for the anniversary of his passing, I'm announcing that I'm donating another five thousand dollars to the Frankie Campbell scholarship fund—and oh shit!—I wasn't supposed to say that, was I? So you gotta make believe you didn't hear me, okay? Because I don't want no credit ever, and wanted this to be synonymous, see—"

"*A*-nonymous," I whispered.

"That too," Max said, and he pointed to one of the boxers. "So what are you waiting for? Ring that bell, and let's get to it. But first—Frankie Jr.—you take another bow, okay? You take *two* bows, one for you and one for your father, and you know what? Take one for your mother too, and for your wife, and for your two little kids, and it don't matter where the money comes from, right? The main thing is to use it to give us a chance we wouldn't get otherwise. Like I'd still be chopping up sides of beef, and Horace here, who could have been a champion, folks, let me tell you that—oh Horace had the goods for sure—and Horace, he might be washing pots and pans somewhere but instead he's got a wife and a son who's the smartest kid in California and who's best buddies with my own boy, Max Jr. But for Horace friendship came first, see, and that's another story for another day, so what's important for you to know is that I love Horace like I love my own brothers—only more because he *ain't* my brother, if you get what I mean—and let's have him take a bow for all the great work he does here—!"

People cheered, and the bell clanged, and while I raised my gloved hands in a gesture of thanks and waved to my boxers and well-wishers, Max came at me, hit me two hard punches to the gut, then clipped me on the chin.

"Gotta pay attention, friend," he said. "That bell rang, and when it does you gotta be ready to come out fighting, because my name is Maximilian Adelbert Baer and I was once heavyweight champion of the world, in case nobody told you."

I fell back on the ropes, shook my head to clear it, feigned collapse—as if I were going to fall flat on my face—and when Max put his gloved palms out to catch me, I caught him with a good left hook to the gut, and then a solid roundhouse right.

Max did a wobbly backwards jig across the ring and, beaming with happiness, shouted out so everyone could hear: "See what I mean about what a great fighter he is, and how he got the one thing I never had?" He tapped on the side of his head. "And we all know what that is . . . or ain't."

Then he came at me again, and we sashayed around the ring together, trading feints and jabs, and when the bell clanged to end the round, Max gave me a big hug—"This is a genuine Baer hug, if you get my meaning!" he called out to the crowd—and then he told me to choose a half-dozen fighters, and each of them would get a minute in the ring with him, and if any of them was able to land a glove on *his* gorgeous kisser, he would be rewarded with a kiss from Ilana! I chose six of my best boxers, and one at a time they got in the ring with Max and went at him, but Max skipped and danced around just beyond their reach, and sometimes he leaned back against the ropes and let them come at him, toying with them, slipping punches deftly, and batting away their blows as if swatting away flies. And after he was done with the six boxers, my boys started to urge me to go in against Max and win a kiss from Ilana, and began a chant that grew louder and louder.

"*Ho-race! Ho-race!*" they chanted. "*We want Horace! We want Horace! We want Horace! Ho-race! Ho-race!*"

I started back into the ring, and Max hugged me again, and told the crowd that he couldn't make the same wager with me that he'd made with my boys. And why was that?

"Because Horace here is a happily married man," he said. "He's married to the most wonderful woman in the world, and I'm proud to say she's my friend too, and if she heard that I was responsible for him getting kisses from Ilana, why I'd be in deep soup, my friends."

Everyone laughed, and I was feeling so happy in that moment—proud of my teams, and proud to be Max's friend, and happy the two of us could give and take the way we could—that I was wishing the afternoon would never end. So I did something I had not expected to do. I suggested that we turn the prize for our prizefighting around, and that for every blow Max landed on *my* face, *he* would get a kiss from Ilana.

Max beamed. "Now I've got a wonderful wife and kids too, like Horace, and I'm a married man too—" he said, and paused for a second or two "—but I'm not a fanatic about it."

And then he and I waltzed around the ring for a while, and gave the folks a show they would never forget, and I made sure that, try as he might, Max did not win a single kiss from Ilana.

After Max and I had showered and dressed, and he was done giving out autographs, he and I walked to his car, exchanging news about our wives and our children, and when we were at the car, he put his arms around me and held me close to him.

"You're looking great, Horace," he said, "and I'm glad we got this time to be alone, you and me, because I want you to know something I ain't even told Mary Ellen or the kids, see—because even though I made a joke from it, it was true what the doc said to me about my ticker, so here's what I'm gonna ask you to do. I'm gonna ask you to give me a little more time the next few months, especially when I'm out on the road, so you can keep an eye on me."

"Sure, Max," I said.

"I meant it when I said you're my best friend in the world," he said. "And I know you got your troubles too, so I kept away from your eyes, and I appreciated that you never used them as an excuse for us not to go at each other, because that shows the kind of classy guy you are. You trusted me on that, didn't you?"

"Yes."

"And hey—you were quick as ever with those hands of yours." He faked an uppercut to my chin, and I blocked it. "Like old times, right? You and me shuffling around, everybody cheering us on and loving us to death. And speaking of loving, there's something else I know, 'cause you got a certain look in your eyes I never seen before, and it tells me you're a man *in* love, and I bet I got that right."

This was when I noticed Hawkins standing by the side of the building, between two large trash containers. He was staring at us without trying to hide, and he was holding an envelope.

I turned away. "What did you say?" I asked.

"Nothing important—just that I love you, Horace," he said. "And it ain't that I love *men*, see, but that I love *you*, okay? And with the news I got from my doc this morning, and seeing Frankie Campbell's boy, I figure why hold back now. So I'm saying what I been wanting to say, which is I never loved anyone the way I loved you. None of my wives, and none of the actresses and chorus girls I played patty-cake with, and not even Joleen, but you don't tell her that, okay? I wouldn't want to make her feel bad, or—" he broke off "—it's just that I miss us hanging out together the way we did, on the road and stuff, and me being the crazy man-about-town, and making people happy wherever we went, and you there to keep me out of *real* trouble. I ain't sorry for anything I did in this life, though, good *or* bad. No regrets, Horace, right? I mean, I never wanted to *hurt* nobody, see, and . . ."

He was crying softly, and I realized that until the doctor had warned him about his heart, it had probably never occurred to him that he was going to die some day. I held him close to me, and while I did I began preparing myself for Hawkins.

"Will you be all right?" I asked.

"Oh sure," he said. "Like Ilana says, only in Hungarian, a saying her people got—'Everything's fine except for all this blood pouring out of a hole in my neck.'"

For a brief moment, in return for what he was confiding in me, I considered telling him the truth about me and Joleen. But what would be gained by telling him *now*, I asked myself. Instead, I told him I had been missing him too, and to give my warm regards to Max Jr. and his family.

"And you do know me well, yes, because there is someone now," I added. "It's very unexpected and quite wonderful—in truth, it's as if I've fallen in love for the very first time in my life."

"Yes," Max said. "Sure, Horace. I'm glad for you, but with me, see, it's always been like a hunger that no matter what I eat, I want more, so I just keep eating. Not just for the ladies, or food, or for going out on the town, but for *life*. People say you can't have everything—but hey—I *want* everything!—and the truth is I'm a little bit scared now, that before I get to have it all they're gonna tell me time's up, the show's over, and that's why . . ."

I glanced toward the YMCA. Hawkins was gone, and Ilana was walking toward us, arm in arm with two of my boxers, Leo behind them, the four of them laughing.

"So you be good, and say hi to Joleen and Horace Jr.," Max said, "and I'll call you, and let you take care of me—we got a deal, right?"

"Yes," I said.

"And you tell Joleen I've been thinking about her too."

"Yes."

"You fought good, Horace," he said, and he said good-by to my fighters, gave them a Confucious saying about it being good for a girl to meet a boy in the park, but better for a boy to park meat in a girl, and then he got into his car with Ilana and Leo, and drove away.

Instead of going home, I made my way down to the Embarcadero, and walked along the harbor until I was under the Golden Gate Bridge, after which I meandered side streets I recalled from when Joleen and I had first lived in San Francisco. I walked and I walked, seemingly without purpose, but wound up where I knew I would, at the house Joleen and I had been living in at the time we met Max Baer, and before I could allow memories to wash through me—the sun had gone down by now, and though my visual acuity was weaker than usual at this time of day—I could make out a man standing in the alleyway next to our old house, and I knew it was Hawkins. I was not surprised.

"Got what you want," he said, showing me the envelope. "Had your chance to show me the man today, but you lost it. So now I gonna do what I tell you I gonna do and bring that man down big-time, make myself a dowry like you never got for Joleen."

I hung my head as if I were a defeated man. But I was ready for him. He was determined to destroy Max Baer's life, or to grow wealthy in the attempt, and I was equally determined to do whatever was necessary to keep him from doing so. But, like Max, Hawkins was afflicted with an insatiable hunger, I knew, and once he was done with me, Max, and Joleen, he would surely move on to Horace Jr., Miss Hémon, Mary Ellen, and others.

"Tell me what you want," I said, and glanced around to see if anyone had followed either of us, or was out walking. The neighborhood, to judge from debris in the street and the sorry state of the houses, several of them abandoned, had clearly fallen on hard times. Next to a three-storey Victorian house that was being demolished—two houses away from where ours still stood—there was now an empty lot, and—my good fortune—two dumpsters sitting in it, one of them overflowing with debris.

"Well before we get to that, I tell you about your wife and what she be to me, so we got no secrets between us," he said.

"Tell me," I said.

"Now since I been calling you brother from the time we met, we gonna add to that by telling you that I be brother to Joleen too," he said. "But you know that already, don't you? Because Joleen, you two being close as any brother and sister I know, and she and me getting acquainted again, talking about how we killed our old selves off, made them into new folks—into born-again critters, like they like to say."

This was and was not news to me, but I could not, in the moment, understand for how long this had and had not been so.

"I know that," I said.

"But what you don't know is that she be good to me and *all* her brothers, the old man too, the way she be to you," he said. "She tell you all that, right?"

I said nothing.

"Way I see it, you been a blind man a long time before you get the diabetes," he said. "You been blind all your life, because—"

"What do you want?" I asked.

"The money, man," he said. "I tell you that before. I want the money. You get me the money however you do, maybe from your bumboy Max, all the loot he gets from movies and shit, and I let you know where to bring it, and I give you the pictures, and then I be on my way, you never see me again, and that's a promise."

I could hear Joleen telling me and Max about her brother James, and my only disappointment, I realized, was that I had no container of lye buried nearby. Whereas James had been imaginary, however, Hawkins was real. He was real, I imagined telling Joleen, in the way Abel was real to Cain, and Jacob to Esau, and Isaac to Ishmael, and Joseph to his brothers, and Judas to Jesus. Whether or not he succeeded in doing in Max, the probability that he would continue to shadow me for days, months, or years was a prospect that induced in me a supreme weariness—an overwhelming desire to close my eyes and sleep, and dream, and in my dreams, to tumble into deeper sleep.

"Let me see the pictures," I said.

He laughed. "You think I some dumb nigger, just give them to you and then you conk me out again, you got another think coming," he said. "Anyways, even you beat shit out of me, and take these, there's another envelope I give to somebody, for insurance, like they like to say."

"You're Simon, aren't you," I said.

"Oh yeah, and you get my apologies for me not being the Simon I was when you was a boy—but I had some hard times, wasn't like you, her there feeding you every damned day of your life," he said. "But once I got away, didn't want nobody to know who I was, so I watched you two and done what you done and got me a name with a new life of my own."

"And what happened to our father?"

"He died of the diabetes, like I told you," he said. "Only I helped it along a little bit. Had it coming, stuff he did to us, and bet you agree on that."

"I do."

"The thing is, Joleen—I call her that out of respect—she loved it more than any woman I ever know, used to say it made her blind, ain't that a pisser, given me with my eye, and you with both yours gone soon," he said. "'Oh you screwin' me blind, Simon,' she'd say to me. 'You screwin' me blind'—only what she did with you must have been upside down and inside out, 'cause it make *you* the blind man."

"Let me see the pictures," I said.

"Not on your life," he said.

"Then on yours," I said, and I faked a left to the stomach, rattled him with a solid right to his blind eye. He was ready too, though, and as he staggered backwards, he clicked a knife open, warned me he was quicker than he looked, that he'd used his little friend before and not to ask about the blood it knew in its lifetime. He could give me an eye like his if I wanted, no extra charge.

"You just get me the money, and we be done," he said. "'Cause you got a son now, and we wouldn't want him hurt no ways, and you got a wife who got what I like to call 'family feeling' for us all, and don't know how she go on living, her son have an accident on his way home one night."

"Get him, Max," I said then, and when Hawkins turned around and jabbed the air where he thought Max would be, I hit him with a single rabbit punch to the back of his neck that did most of the job I intended it to do.

He lay there, lifeless, though his heart continued to beat. I opened the envelope and there was nothing in it but a sports page from the *San Francisco Examiner* with an article about Willie Mays and the San Francisco Giants. I was not surprised. I lifted Hawkins, draped one of his arms over my shoulder, and walked with him to the empty lot as if walking a drunken friend home. When we got to the dumpsters, I laid him on the ground, took out my syringe, lifted his sleeve, filled the syringe with air, found a vein, and injected the air.

He twitched, but only two or three times, and a minute later, I took two steps up the metal rungs on the side of the dumpster that was mostly empty, and heaved him up and over the edge. I walked away, checking out garages until I found a gas can next to a lawn-mower. I borrowed the can, went to the dumpster, poured the gasoline in on Hawkins. Then I lit the envelope that had no pictures in it, and dropped it into the dumpster. A few seconds later, the flames whooshed and rose, and I tossed the syringe in, and before the sun rose, I knew—something I would love to have been able to say to Max, because he was a man who appreciated bad jokes as well as good ones—Simon Abraham, good son of the South that he was, would be gone with the wind. And who will miss you? I heard myself ask. Who will care?

When I arrived home, Joleen did not ask me why I was late or where I had been—she rarely did—and she set out dinner for the two of us. She did ask how the event at the YMCA had gone, but I told her it had gone well, and that Max had asked about her and Horace Jr.

"Simon will not bother us anymore," I said.

"Simon?

"Our brother," I said.

"Then you know," she said.

"Oh yes," I said. "But we had a talk, and I persuaded him to leave San Francisco and never return."

"You saw to that?"

"I did."

"Whatever he told you about us, you should take with the proverbial grain of salt."

"Not a pillar of salt?"

"I am not Lot's wife—or your wife either, for that matter," she said.

"True enough," I said.

"I've never been one to look back."

"Of course."

"He was a nasty man, like our father," she said. "He led a pitiable life, and against my better judgment, I felt sorry for him at times—blood is blood, Horace—and I probably should have told you about him years ago."

"He's gone now," I said.

"A ghost become a ghost?" she asked.

"You might say that," I said.

"Then I thank you for seeing that he will not haunt us anymore," she said. "You must feel relieved."

"Oh yes," I said.

"In truth, I didn't know what to say when he came calling and made himself known to me, for if he hadn't made himself known to me, I would not have recognized him," she said. "What to do, I kept thinking. What to do. But everything that came to mind would, in my mind, have only made things worse. So I did nothing." She gave me a half smile. "I *am* sorry, Horace, but seeing Max today must have been a joy, and you have been looking quite good of late—remarkably good, in fact. Despite Hawkins, and the diabetes, and living with me and my clouded moods, I have never seen you looking better, and that makes me happy."

I sensed her meaning. "You don't mind?" I asked.

"No," she said. "I am pleased you're happy—and also relieved of certain feelings—responsibilities, yes?—I have carried with me for too many years. And I can think of us again in the way we were before we truly knew one another—when you would sometimes call me your dove."

I took her hand in mine, and recited a line we knew well. "'I sleep, but my heart waketh: it is the voice of my beloved that knocketh . . . my dove, my undefiled: for my head is filled with dew, and my locks with the drops of the night.'"

"Yes," she said. "And do you know why the lover calls his beloved a dove?"

"Because when doves mate, they mate for life," I said. "Horace Jr. explained that to me."

"That is good news," Joleen said.

"Good news because you and I are *not* doves?"

"Perhaps."

"But did you ever hear the joke Max would make in one of his routines with Maxie Rosenbloom, about what happens in Mississippi and Louisiana when a couple get divorced?" I asked.

"No," she said. "Tell me—what happens in Mississippi and Louisiana when a couple get divorced?"

"They're still permitted to remain brother and sister," I said.

Joleen's smile vanished. "You have a cruel streak in you too, Horace," she said. "Unlike Max, however, you have kept it contained for the most part, and it has proven its usefulness on more than one occasion, as it has today. I trust it will continue to serve you well. And I'm grateful that Max had the good sense not to have told this particular joke in my presence. It is of no ultimate concern, of course. He does not know, and never will, am I correct?"

"You are correct."

"Please," she said. "Promise me. No matter how or why you are tempted—there is no reason on earth ever to trouble him. Promise me."

The next morning I went to the Lighthouse, and I told Miss Duncan that Hawkins had asked me to tell her he was leaving town—had already left, in fact—and that though he was grateful to her and the Lighthouse for all they had done for him, he would not be returning. I said he had given me his new address, and I asked her for the envelope he had given her for safekeeping, and told her I would forward it to him.

Her hand trembling, she took a sealed envelope from a drawer in her desk, and gave it to me. I opened the envelope in her presence, and found three grainy photographs of me and Max lying in bed, Max's head resting on my shoulder, the two of us smiling smiles of contentment. I asked Miss Duncan if there were any other copies of these photos in existence, and she said that to her knowledge there were not, and she crossed her heart and swore to me on her mother's grave that she had not known what was in the envelope, only that Hawkins had entrusted it to her. I took several of her necklaces in my fist, used them to pull her toward me, and informed her that if she broke her vow I would see to it that she would leave town as Hawkins had. I was, I assured her, a man of my word.

I brought the envelope upstairs to Miss Hémon, and I told her what I had told Joleen—that I had had a talk with Hawkins and had persuaded him to leave town and never return.

"You are more enterprising than I gave you credit for," she said.

"Did you know about this?" I asked, showing her the envelope.

"Yes, but there's nothing in there—just an old newspaper."

"That's correct," I said.

She sighed. "Oh Horace, I hear by your voice—too cold, too cold by far—that your affection for me is fading, and I hope you will tell me this is not so." She leaned against me, her hand light on the small of my back.

"I have nothing *but* affection for you," I said.

"But as to the expression *of* your affection . . . ?"

"You and Hawkins were friends in the way we have been friends, is that not so?"

"Does it matter?"

"Under the aspect of eternity, as Horace Jr. might say, nothing matters," I said. "But to me, yes, it matters."

"You are a gentle soul, Horace," she said. "You deserve better than you have received, and I am trying with all my heart to give you what you deserve—what I believe you *need*—and what I know *I* need. I will not dissemble or be coy. You are an extraordinary man, and it is my good fortune that we found one another."

"Any other man would have loved you as I have, and . . ." I began.

"And many have—is that what you were about to say?"

I did not reply.

"But yours is not the right way of thinking about it," she said. "Perhaps with time you will see that, and we can be friends again, for it is you I love and not any other man, and I love you in this time and in this place, and I will miss you terribly if . . ."

"We will do the best we can," I said.

"Perhaps," she said. "Most people, most of the time, do *not* do the best they can, it seems to me. Most people disappoint us in the end, as I have disappointed you."

"That is because of a flaw in my character that is beyond repair," I said. "Still, I will say what I have been thinking and do not wish to hide—that I have never known, or expected to know, a sweetness with anyone such as the sweetness I have known with you."

She spoke quickly, as if she had been rehearsing her words: "You made that possible by who you are," she said. "You have a large capacity for kindness, nor have you let your wounds, such as they are, get in the way of our friendship." She exhaled. "And now tell me about your friend Max Baer, whom you saw yesterday."

"He will need me to be near him in the months to come," I said. "He is not well."

"And after that?"

"We will see what we will see."

She kissed me, her lips grazing mine, and then she touched my lips with her fingers, as if she were about to begin reading words there.

"From what you have told me, your friend Max and I are not unlike one another," she said. "Apparently, we both believe in taking as much pleasure for ourselves in this life as we can, and though we both fear hurting others, we rarely let this fear govern our actions."

She stepped away, went to her desk. "Will you and Joleen join us for dinner this Friday evening?" she asked. "The children are expecting you and will be disappointed if you do not come. They hope Horace Jr. will come too."

"We will be there," I said, surprised to hear the words come from my mouth.

"That pleases me, Mister Littlejohn," she said. "And even in Hawkins Johnson's absence, you will continue to come to the Lighthouse so that we may be of service to you, yes?"

"I hope so," I said.

"I am, again, pleased and, I must admit, happily surprised," she said. "So I will now tell you something I have thought of telling you for a long time, not by way of explanation or rationalization, I trust, but simply because it is something my mother said frequently when I was growing up that I want you to know."

"Please."

"Like Anna and David, I never knew who my father was, though my mother had many friends who stayed with us—men I called 'uncle'—and when I would ask about them, for they were a motley bunch for the most part, and I could not understand why she tolerated them and was kind to them—she would say to me, in French, and I translate loosely, 'So much pleasure for them, and so little pain for me, don't you see, my darling?' "

I said nothing.

"*Do* you see, Horace?"

"Possibly," I said.

"*Possibly?*" she said.

"Didn't you once assure me that it is good to know that we live in the land of possibility and not the land of probability?" I said.

"I'm glad Hawkins is gone, and I thank you," she said. "Joleen will be glad to hear the news too, I am certain, if she has not already received it."

"She has," I said.

She went to the door and locked it, then returned and kissed me again, more fully, with her lips and her fingers, and I chose not to resist. What surprised me, especially given my age—I would be forty-nine years old within a few months—was that the more I knew her, the more inflamed was my passion for her. Although I delighted in her in the way, as in The Song of Solomon, the young lovers delighted in one another's flesh, I believed that my desire for her was becoming infinitely more intense than a young person could imagine.

"As for us," she said, "the way I see things, we should forgive ourselves—always, always—for acts, for thoughts, and for feelings that have the potential to make us feel ashamed, or guilty, or do us harm. But we should *never* forgive others for harmful things they do to us. Do you agree?"

"Perhaps."

When she kissed me the next time, I searched out the small scar on her lower lip, tugged on it with my teeth.

"Do you agree now?" she asked.

"More than I did a minute ago."

"I am not one to theorize about love," she said, "or about much else—but I do believe that this—what I have just said—is at the heart of what can strengthen friendship and love between two people."

"To forgive ourselves—always always—but never to forgive others?"

"Ah, you are my very best student, Mister Littlejohn," she said. "I was right in having seen your potential and in having encouraged it. As Miss Duncan might put it, you do *see* what I mean, don't you."

"Possibly," I said.

Coda

*Awake, O north wind; and come, thou
south; blow upon my garden, that the
spices thereof may flow out. Let my
beloved come into his garden, and eat his
pleasant fruits. (4:16)*

On the day Max Baer died, November 21, 1959, he and I were staying at the Hollywood Roosevelt Hotel, near studios where Max was scheduled to film several television commercials. Two days earlier, after Max had refereed a boxing match in Phoenix, Arizona, we had driven to Garden Grove, California, so that he could keep a promise he had made thirteen years earlier to Tommy Owen, the son of Max's prime sparring partner, Jerry "Curly" Owen (a man who possessed total recall of the Bible, and would become self-appointed chaplain to every boxer and wrestler in America), that when the boy turned eighteen he would give him a car for a birthday present. And so Max had kept his promise and had had a gorgeous mint green MGA 1500 Sports Coupé delivered to the boy's home while we visited with him to celebrate his coming of age. I had made the arrangements.

Several months before this, on June 3, 1959, Max had sat beside me and Joleen at Horace Jr.'s graduation from the University of California at Berkeley, just as, two days before that, Joleen and I had sat beside him, Mary Ellen, and their family, at Max Jr.'s graduation from Santa Clara University. Max and I were as proud on these occasions as any two fathers could be, for the years between Max's retirement from professional boxing and the college graduations of our sons had for the most part been kind to us. And nothing in this life, he would often tell me—not the championship, his carousing, or his affairs—could compare with the pleasure he took from seeing his boy grow into a man. Nor, at the graduations, and the celebrations at the home in Sacramento that followed—and this was before Max's final appearance at the YMCA, and the fateful events of that day—did Max, true gentleman that he could often be, ever indicate in any way, either to me or to Horace Jr., whether in jest or by innuendo, that Horace Jr. might be the son of any other man but me.

By this time, although the boys were, as they as had been at the ranch and were again at the home in Sacramento, inseparable—and although they would often spend time with one another during school vacations and summers—they had, in their interests, and in the careers that would follow from these interests, diverged.

Max Baer Jr., who had majored in business administration and minored in philosophy, began, through an introduction from one of Max's friends, an acting career in London, where, at the Blackpool Pavillion several months after his graduation, he starred in a production of *Goldilocks and the Three Bears*. After this his life was consumed, primarily, with acting, and his early success as Jethro Bodine in *The Beverly Hillbillies*, though providing him with the kind of visibility most actors yearn for, also typecast him in a way that did not allow him the diversity of roles he wished for. Putting his business acumen to work, however, he began producing films that became great financial successes, beginning with *Macon County Line,* in which he also starred, and which film was, for a quarter of a century, the highest grossing movie per dollar ever made. Though a man large in body and spirit, Max Baer Jr. was also, like his father, a man with a surprisingly gentle disposition.

As for Horace Jr., his love of the Bible, and, more, his passion to learn how it had come into being, was there from his earliest years—an obsession that knew no rivals. At the same time, he had a mind that, when not consumed with wanting to know *everything* about anything that was of interest to him, was also playful in ways that continually astonished.

Thus, for example, while enrolled in a course at the University of California in Bible history, he chose to write a paper on the origins of the story of Abraham and Isaac—the famous Akedah, wherein Abraham is called upon to sacrifice his only son, Isaac, to God—he produced an essay which so impressed his professor, himself a renowned biblical scholar, that the professor encouraged Horace to submit the essay to a prestigious scholarly journal. Horace did what the professor said, and the essay was accepted for publication—this when Horace was but nineteen years old—and was already in page proofs when Horace Jr. alerted his professor to the fact that he had invented virtually all the alleged Hebraic and Egyptian sources he had cited. When the professor asked Horace what in the world could have possessed him to have done such a thing, Horace said he thought it would be something Isaac's son, Jacob—the original "trickster" of Jewish lore—might have wanted him to do.

At this point the professor ordered Horace to depart from his presence and never again to wave a red flag in his face, yet when Horace started walking away, the professor summoned him back, and the two of them, according to Horace, laughed uproariously while the professor told Horace that this proved his instinct correct: Horace had everything a true scholar needed to succeed—splendid research skills, an admirable work ethic, a passion for his subject, a felicitous prose style, and—above all—what was lacking in most biblical scholars—imagination.

Less than an hour after we had risen from bed on the morning of November 21, Max came into our sitting room from the bathroom, where he had been shaving, and complained of pains in his chest. Did I recall his having fallen in the last few days? Could the pain be the result of the light bare-knuckled sparring we had engaged in before sleep in our Phoenix hotel room three nights before? Despite the high life Max favored, I knew of no man who kept himself in such splendid physical shape. Although he had given up professional boxing nearly two decades before, he still weighed the same as he had weighed when he defeated Carnera for the heavyweight championship, and he still had the thirty-two-inch waist and Adonis-like physique that had been the envy of other men, and the ideal my young boxers aspired to.

I was concerned, of course, and suggested we have a doctor summoned to our room. To my surprise, not only did Max not resist my suggestion but, wiping shaving cream from his face with a towel, he took the phone from my hand, and asked for a doctor. The desk clerk said he would send a house doctor up right away.

"A *house* doctor?" Max said. "No, dummy—I need a *people* doctor."

Max walked into the bedroom, lay down, and closed his eyes. I took his hand in mine, and felt his pulse, which, though strong, was much slower than usual.

"I been thinking about Joe Louis," Max said, "and of the licking

I took from him, and what I been thinking is that no matter what anyone says, the truth is I was licked by a better man."

"But Max," I began, "when you were in your prime . . ."

"Nah," he said. "You're just trying to make me feel good, Horace, and hey, I'd do the same if you were lying here like me and had all these bozos hammering on your chest the way they're banging on mine. The truth is, see, Louis was a better man. Pound for pound, there weren't nobody I ever fought against or seen as good as him. I hear he's been having his troubles, though—that they locked him up in a loony bin for a while, so you wish him well for me next time you see him, okay?"

And saying this, he sat up and announced that he was feeling better. "Hey—glad to get that off my chest, right?"

He laughed at his joke, then went to the door to let in a man who, black bag in hand, introduced himself as Doctor Edward S. Koziol.

Max sat on the side of the bed, and the doctor listened to his chest with a stethoscope, said that he was concerned about what he was hearing, and gave Max several pills. I poured a glass of water for Max, who swallowed the pills. A moment later, the glass fell from his hand, he grabbed at the doctor's arms, and said the pains—and the pressure, as if soldiers were marching across his chest—were getting worse.

"It's really killing me, Doc," he said, bent over but forcing a smile. "Know what I mean?"

Max lay down again, his eyes shut tight, his brow furrowed, then sat halfway up and tried to suck in large quantities of air. A fire department rescue squad, having been summoned by the desk clerk, arrived a few minutes later, and began administering oxygen. As soon as Max was breathing more easily, he stood, and once again declared that he was feeling better.

"Hey, Doc," he said while circling the room, first one way and then the other. "Did you hear the one about the husband who comes home and finds his wife in bed with her doctor? 'It's not what you think,' the doctor says. 'I was taking your wife's temperature.' 'Oh yeah?' the husband replies. 'Well let me tell you this, Doc—when you pull that thing out, it better have numbers on it!'"

The doctor did not laugh, and neither did I. Max shrugged, after which all color drained from his face. "Oh God, here I go," he said and, his face a sudden, ghostly shade of blue, he fell onto the bed, and was gone.

Max was buried in a garden crypt in St Mary's Lawn Cemetery in Sacramento. Along with Jack Dempsey, Joe Louis, Max Baer Jr., Buddy, and Augie, I was honored to be one of the pallbearers. Several thousand people attended the funeral, and in recognition of Max's World War Two service, an American Legion rifle squad ended the ceremony by firing three dry volleys into the air. Max was fifty years old.

Only on the second morning following his burial did I notice that Joleen had carved a small Star of David into the headboard of our bed, a bed she and I have slept in ever since, even to the day upon which she has been setting down these words.

About the Author

JAY NEUGEBOREN is the author of
21 previous books, including award-winning novels (*The Stolen
Jew, Before My Life Began, Poli:A Mexican Boy in Early Texas,
1940*. and *The American Sun & Wind Moving Picture Company*),
non-fiction (*Imagining Robert, Transforming Madness*), and four
collections of prize-winning stories. His essays and stories have appeared in many publications, including *The New York Review of
Books, The Atlantic Monthly, The American Scholar, Psychiatric
Services, Black Clock, Ploughshares, Commonweal, Moment, Ha-
dassah*, and *The New York Times*, and have been reprinted in more
than 50 anthologies, including *Best American Short Stories* and
O. Henry Prize Stories. The recipient of numerous awards, including fellowships from the Guggenheim Foundation and the National
Endowment for the Arts, he was Professor and Writer-in-Residence
for many years at The University of Massachusetts at Amherst, and
has also taught at Stanford, Columbia, and the State University of
New York at Old Westbury. He now lives and writes in New York
City, where he is on the faculty of the Writing Program of the Graduate School of the Arts at Columbia University.